STONEHILL
BOOK SIX

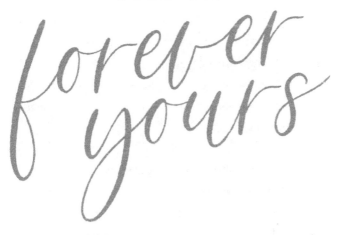

forever yours

Joanne #6 of 6
5/21
BK 1-22

Cover design by Okay Creations
Book layout by Lori Colbeck

ISBN-13: 978-1-950348-16-9

STONEHILL
BOOK SIX

forever yours

MARCI
BOLDEN

PINK SAND
— PRESS —

CHAPTER ONE

*A*iden Howard's stomach clenched into a bundle of nerves as he parked in front of the O'Connell Realty office. He had sworn that once he spread his wings in "the real world," he'd never come back to this sleepy little suburb. Yet, here he was. Not only had he returned to the small town where he grew up, but he was committing to staying for the long-term by purchasing a home.

Part of him wanted to run before it was too late. But it was already too late. He'd accepted a job at Stonehill Hospital. He'd already crammed what he'd brought back from New York City into his parents' garage. He had told people he was coming home. His cousin Phil and his wife were expecting a new baby in just over a month, and Aiden had promised to be here to help them out.

He had broken a lot of promises in the past. But he had come home to change. His mom liked to talk about how they were a tight-knit family, but the truth was the rifts ran deep and wide.

Living away from home, moving to the city, had taken a toll on Aiden that he hadn't even begun to process yet. He just knew he needed time to heal his soul after the horrors he'd seen. He wasn't soft by any means, but he sure as hell hadn't been prepared to deal with the level of inhumanity he'd faced on a near-daily basis.

So, despite years of swearing he never would, he'd come back to the security of suburban life. Not only was he back, but he was taking steps to settle in for the long haul. After taking a deep breath to firm up his resolve, Aiden climbed out of his SUV and walked into the office. He smiled warmly at the receptionist and let her know he had an appointment with Mallory Martinson-Canton. Within moments, she came out of her office, pregnant belly first, and beckoned for him to join her.

Aiden tried to keep his physician's mind turned off when he wasn't in the emergency room, but he couldn't help noticing Mallory's slow movements. He'd only been back in town for a week and didn't know Mallory well, but he was uneasy with the obvious toll this pregnancy was taking on her. "You look tired."

She turned her lips down in an exaggerated frown as she sat behind her desk. "Nice to see you too."

"Sorry." He wasn't really. "How are you feeling?"

She shifted in her chair. "Have you ever seen one of those stores where you make your own stuffed animals?"

Aiden blinked. "Sure."

"Have you ever seen one of those stuffed animal skins get filled to the point of bursting?"

He grinned, finally following her train of thought. "You're only eight months along, Mal. You've got a bit more filling out to do."

Even though she insisted she was miserable, she smiled and happiness lit her eyes. "I'm going to explode. I swear it." She rolled her head back and sighed dramatically. "How are you doing?"

He blew out a breath to release some of his stress. He'd been home a week. A very long week. "I love my mom."

Mallory's grin widened. "But?"

"But we need to get moving on this house search."

Aiden knew Mallory understood and wasn't judging him. His mom and Mallory's mother-in-law Kara were cousins, and they weren't on the best of terms. Whenever Aiden mentioned Phil, Becca would mutter under her breath about how Kara had torn their family apart. Mending those familial rifts wasn't going to be easy. Becca Howard was almost as good at holding a grudge as Kara Canton.

Almost.

The cousins were more alike than they wanted to admit. Both were fiercely protective of their kids and would do anything to help them, but both seemed to be a little put out that Aiden and Phil were trying to help them let go of past grievances and move on.

"First things first." Mallory slid a clipboard and pen across to him. "All of our clients have to have a background check. Even family."

Aiden didn't protest. Mallory's mom had been hurt in an attempted mugging a few years ago and still suffered side effects from the injury. He was happy that the company was enforcing rules to protect their agents. As he filled out the form, she tossed questions at him.

How many bedrooms? How many bathrooms? Was location important?

He knew the answers to all of those without thinking about them. As soon as he had started to realize city living wasn't for him, he found himself dreaming of the home he'd have some day. Three bedrooms. At least two full bathrooms. A big fenced yard. Preferably a two-story home with an open layout downstairs to make entertaining easier.

He wasn't a great cook, but he loved the idea of having big family dinners or lots of friends over. During his time in New York, he'd become a bit of a hermit. The stresses of working in an ER hadn't left him with enough energy to socialize. He'd always been active and involved, but leaving Stonehill had changed him in more ways than one. He needed to get back to living his life instead of just getting through each day.

He hadn't quite determined what that life was going to look like. When he'd left Stonehill, he'd still been too immature to thoroughly understand what his future should be. While in New York, he had become too isolated to care. He was determined to do better now, and that meant having room for big gatherings. Even if he couldn't cook a proper meal for them.

"Hey, Mal," a familiar voice called.

Aiden froze. He knew that voice. The melodic tone had haunted his dreams ever since he left Stonehill. Whenever he'd had a particularly bad day, he'd close his eyes and dig into the depths of his memory just to hear that voice.

"Marcus has left for the day. Can you— Oh." The sound of her approaching footsteps stopped as abruptly as the woman's words. "I'm sorry. I didn't realize you had a client."

With his breath lodged in his chest like wet cement, Aiden spun in his chair. He couldn't stop himself. Just as he suspected, Megumi Tanaka had stopped in her tracks and was staring at him. She still had the long black hair he remembered, but her glasses were gone. She'd planned on getting surgery to correct her vision because she couldn't stand to wear contacts and hated wearing glasses. She must have followed through.

She was slimmer now too, more fit. He had tried to get her to go to the gym with him for the two years they had dated in college, but she was committed to her studies. Studies that were supposed to lead her to being an obstetrician. Why was she here? At a realty office?

She stared at him, her thin lips parted, as she widened her eyes. She was obviously just as stunned to see him.

"It's not problem," Mallory said. "This is Phil's cousin—"

"Aiden," Meg said.

The last time he'd heard her say his name was when he ended their relationship without warning. He hadn't told her that he'd applied for a residency in New York because he hadn't expected to get it. When he had, he couldn't turn it down and he couldn't expect Meg to give up her life to go with him. At least that was the reasoning he'd used for leaving her behind.

He'd insisted ending their relationship had been the best thing for both of them. Only later had he realized that they could have worked around their separation, like she'd told him they could, if he'd been willing to put in the effort. Maybe he wouldn't have felt so overwhelmed by his residency if he'd let Meg be there for him. When his life had started falling apart, she was the first person he'd wanted to reach out to. She'd always been able to talk him through his problems. But he'd burned that bridge—and blown it up for good measure—before he left.

Four years later, she stood before him, and even though he had no right, his first instinct was to wrap her in his arms and hug her tight. He stood and took a step toward her before realizing that was a terrible idea.

"Hi, Meg," he said hesitantly when she lifted one brow at him in what appeared to be a silent warning for him to keep his distance.

"You're Phil's cousin?"

"Well. We're *second* cousins if we're getting technical about it." He smiled.

She didn't. "The one moving back from..."

He shoved his hands in his pockets. He didn't know why he was surprised that she was less than happy to see him. "New York. The city just didn't work out like I'd planned."

Meg stared at him as if she didn't know what to say next. She could say she told him so. Because she had. When she'd asked him not to break up with her, she'd told him that he wasn't being realistic about what the city was like. She'd told him he wasn't going to be living out some sitcom where he and his closest friends would hang out sipping coffee between grand efforts to save a life. The city was brutal and cold and real. She'd told him he wasn't ready for that.

She had been right. He hadn't been ready, and the reality had nearly destroyed his sanity.

Mallory broke the tense silence. "You two know each other?"

The hard edge that filled Meg's eyes was like a knife to Aiden's heart. Four years may have passed, but she looked as angry now as she had when he'd told her he was leaving Stonehill without her.

"No. Not really," Meg said coolly. "I didn't mean to interrupt your meeting."

"Meg," Mallory called. "You needed something?"

"I'll catch you later," she stated and disappeared.

Aiden watched her leave, his spirit sinking with every step she took. Somewhere in the back of his mind, he'd thought he might run into his ex-girlfriend, but he hadn't expected that to happen here. Or so soon after his return. He'd thought he'd have time to brace himself for that moment.

"You want to tell me what that was about?" Mallory asked.

Aiden's gut twisted with guilt. "We dated in med school. It didn't end well. Obviously."

Mallory started at him, her eyes widening much the way Meg's had done when she'd spotted him. "Oh. My. God. You're the one... You left to do your residency without her?"

He didn't have to answer. The horror on her face made it clear she understood exactly why Meg had such a bad reaction to seeing him.

sh

By the time Meg reached her office, she was trembling like a scared child. In a way, she guessed she was. Aiden Howard had been her first real relationship and her first real heartbreak. She had foolishly believed they would spend the rest of their lives together, right up to the moment he said they wouldn't. She hadn't seen that coming.

Admittedly, she'd been naïve in the ways of men and romance before she somehow ended up in a relationship with Aiden. They'd both been students. They'd understood the stress they were both under. They both had parents pressuring them to succeed. They had shared a strong connection that Meg had thought was unbreakable.

Until he broke it.

Since Meg was a year behind him, they had talked many times about what would happen when it was time for him to do his residency. Not once had they talked about him breaking up with her so he could go boldly into the future alone. She'd been shocked. She hadn't known he'd even applied to New York. He'd given her a long list of excuses: he thought it was best if they ended things so he could start fresh when he got there, long-distance relationships didn't work, they weren't ready for the long-term commitment they'd talked about. And a dozen other reasons she hadn't expected to hear.

They all had boiled down to one thing: Aiden had turned his back on the future they had planned.

She had done her best to forget him, but he was always there, lingering in the back of her mind. Now he was back. And related to Mallory—Meg's best friend and coworker. Perfect.

Sinking into her chair, Meg tightened her hands into fists, trying to stop them from shaking. That hadn't eased her nerves a bit when her office door opened. She knew it was Mallory before her friend squeezed into the small space that was Meg's office.

"I didn't know," Mallory said, closing the door behind her. "I swear, I didn't know."

"It's not your fault." Meg forced herself to swallow when her voice quivered.

"I didn't put the pieces together, Meg. I'm just..." She waved her had. "My head is a million miles away right now. I'm so sorry." Mallory wriggled her way into the straight-back chair across from Meg, her eyes filled with what looked like guilt. "I know how much he hurt you."

"You couldn't have known. You and I met *after* Aiden left. I probably never even said his name after what happened."

"Are you okay?"

Meg looked at her hands. They were still trembling. "I will be. I just need a few minutes." She inhaled deeply before the tears threatening to fill her eyes could take hold. "He's moving back?"

Mallory nodded but then was quiet for too long before saying, "You know how Phil grew up without knowing his family?"

Meg braced herself. "Yes."

"It's really important to him that he reconnect with them," Mal said with sympathetic undertones. "But you're family too," she quickly added. "You're like the sister I never had. You know that."

Meg felt the same about Mallory. Except Meg had an older sister. She and Aya had never been close, though. Meg was the black sheep of the Tanaka clan. She'd been so young when they left Japan and had become the most Westernized of them. Even though her parents had tried, their traditions had never taken root with Meg. She felt a closer bond to Mallory than she ever had to Aya. Because of that close bond, she knew where this conversation was going and decided to save Mallory some stress and tears.

"So. Aiden will be around quite a bit, then," Meg said.

Mallory nodded, and Meg wanted to cry from the sense of betrayal she felt. Not at Mallory or Phil. More at life in general. At the universe. At the cruelty of the fates. She'd never gotten over the hurt Aiden had caused her. She'd buried it, denied it, ignored it. But she'd never gotten over it. Now she had no choice but to face it. She dug in, tapping into that false bravado she used so often.

"I was shocked to see him," she said. "But now that I know he's in town and that we might run into each other, I won't have such a bad reaction next time."

"I don't want to add salt to your wounds, Meg."

Meg shrugged. "Aiden and I broke up a long time ago. My wounds are healed."

Mallory stared at her. If anyone could know how much of a lie that was, it would be Mallory. Meg had moved in with Mallory not long after Aiden left Stonehill. They'd gone through a lot of wine and even more tissues their first few months of living together. Just a few years later and Mallory was happily married, while Meg kept men as far away from her as possible. She had no intention of going through that kind of heartache again. She took in Mallory's expression of obvious disbelief.

"Okay," Meg amended. "My wounds aren't *healed*, but they are old enough that I have to get over it. And I will. Aiden is part of your family now. I'll have to see him from time to time. I can do that."

"I would never ask—"

"Hey," Meg interjected with a forced smile. "I'm a big girl. I can tolerate running into him at the occasional gathering."

Mallory wrung her hands, obviously still unsettled. She wasn't the only one, but as she always did, Meg set her feelings aside.

"What happened with Aiden and me was a long time ago, Mal. Maybe this is the kick in the ass I needed to finally move on." She shrugged. "It'll be fine. Really."

CHAPTER TWO

$\mathcal{M}$eg tried to keep her balance on the ice-covered sidewalk leading to Mallory's front porch. When she reached the stairs, she clung to the handrail, easing her way to the front door. Finally, she reached her goal and pressed the doorbell several times, conveying her urgent need to get inside the warmth of their home.

Phil looked confused as he opened the door, and she suspected Mallory forgot to tell him Meg was coming for dinner. Mallory was forgetting a lot of things these days. Although Meg hadn't become an obstetrician like she'd planned, she knew Mallory's changing hormones impacted her hippocampus, resulting in lapses of memory. Understanding the cause did little to ease Mallory's frustrations, but Meg appreciated the opportunity to utilize the education she'd cut short.

Meg squeezed past Phil into the warmth of his home. "You need to put salt on your sidewalk."

He closed the door. "You didn't fall, did you?"

She shook her head as she shrugged out of her coat. "I have impeccable balance. Even on ice."

"Good." He took her coat and hung it on the hook by the wall. "Mal told me about—"

Meg lifted her hand before he could say the name that had been rolling through her mind all afternoon and evening. "Don't worry about it."

"Well, it's just that…" His words faded as the front door opened.

Just as she'd done earlier in the day, Meg froze as she came face-to-face with Aiden.

He stopped too, but he managed to give her a weak smile. "Hey. I didn't know you were coming for dinner."

Her stomach knotted. He was here for dinner too?

Holding up a bag from the little grocery store a few blocks away, he said, "Mal forgot to get garlic bread. We can't have lasagna without garlic bread."

"Oh, no," Meg said, her voice holding the same sharp edge she'd heard come from her lips earlier. "We certainly can't."

Phil hesitantly grabbed the bag. "I'll take this to the kitchen. You two…be nice," he muttered before rushing from the room.

Meg realized she'd ground her teeth together and had to force her jaw to relax. "I didn't know you were going to be here."

"Uh, Phil invited me. Last minute. I'm sure he didn't know you were going to be here. I can go."

"No," Meg said quickly. She bit at her lip, trying to get control of her mouth. "Look. This is awkward. For both of us. But Phil is your cousin and Mallory is my best friend. They're about to have a baby, so…" She exhaled harshly. "So we're going to see each other and we need to deal with that."

"I don't want to make you uncomfortable." He sounded sincere, which softened her anger a bit.

"Well, this is uncomfortable, and we're just going to have to work through it. We're adults, Aiden," she said with a conviction that she didn't feel, but she'd be damned if she would admit how shaken she was at seeing him again. "What happened between us was a long time ago. We just have to work through the awkwardness."

He frowned and shoved his hands in his pockets. That was the same uneasy posture he'd taken moments before shattering her heart four years ago. "When I saw you at the office yesterday," he started.

Her heart twisted around in her chest, waiting for him to continue. He didn't have the power to hurt her anymore—she had nothing left that he could take—but the anxiety still built in her chest.

"I was surprised to see you. I thought at some point that I might seek you out, but I wasn't expecting to see you. I wanted to apologize to you," he said. "I *want* to apologize to you."

"For?"

The already thick tension between them increased. "For leaving the way I did. I know I hurt you. I am so sorry for that. And I want you to know...it wasn't you."

Meg lifted her brows before she snorted a sarcastic, disbelieving laugh. "I know it wasn't me, Aiden. I never, for one moment, thought it was *me*." Her anger reignited, she let the words tumble unchecked. "It was you and your stupid blow-smoke-up-my-ass attitude that made you think you were too good for this town and everyone in it, including me. It was that Golden Boy ego that your parents instilled in you. Oh my God." She laughed and shook her head. "You know what hurt me? Not that you left. What hurt me was the way you did it. Without warning or notice. Just, 'See ya, Meg. Thanks for being my doormat for the last two years.'"

He widened his eyes and jerked back as if she'd struck him. "That's not what you were."

"Really? Then what was I?"

He opened his mouth, but no words came out.

"Yeah," she said when his silence proved her point. "You used me."

"I didn't."

"You did."

The muscles in his jaw tensed as he continued to stare at her. He furrowed his brow and pressed his lips into a thin line, seemingly angered by her accusation.

"The moment you no longer needed a chemistry tutor and a bed warmer, you were gone."

"That's—"

"Completely accurate. Don't bother trying to tell me I was more than that."

"You were."

She didn't mean her voice to sound so broken, but her pain was obvious when she asked, "Then why did you walk away?"

"I'm sorry."

She wanted to believe him, but she'd been fooled by his sad act more than once when they were dating. Instead of caving, she rolled her eyes and looked away. "I'm sure."

"I am. I've grown up, Meg."

She considered his words for a moment. "I hope so, Aiden. I certainly hope so because you had plenty of growing up to do. I'm going to go see if Mallory needs help."

She marched toward the kitchen without looking back.

sh

Aiden felt like an outsider as the small gathering sat around the table.

Meg and Phil's daughter Jessica sat next to each other, chattering with the ease of old friends while Mallory and Phil sat side by side with the comfort their marriage afforded them. Aiden sat at the end of the table by himself. He was determined to be part of his family, but the casual interactions between everyone else was a reminder that he didn't belong.

"The lasagna looks delicious, Mal," he said, attempting to insert himself into the conversation.

"Grandma made it," Jessica announced. She spoke slowly, enunciating her words so he could understand her. Her Down syndrome could make it hard for people to decipher her words when she talked too quickly, and apparently she'd noticed. Eventually he'd spend enough time around her that he could keep up with her usual mile-a-minute chatter.

"Hey," Mallory stated, shocked. "I baked it."

"But Grandma put it together and told you *how* to bake it."

Without thinking, Aiden said, "Have you ever had Meg's lasagna? It's pretty good."

Jessica looked from Meg to Aiden and then back. "How does he know that?"

Meg winked at Jessica. "Because my cooking is legendary, sweetie. I'm famous all around the world for my amazing culinary skills."

Jessica widened her eyes. "*Wow.*"

"Don't lie to the child," Mallory chastised.

Aiden cleared his throat. "Uh, Meg and I used to be really good friends before I moved away. I ate her cooking sometimes."

"All the time. He doesn't cook," Meg said to her little friend.

"Lots of men don't," Jessica said, as if she would know. "The only reason Daddy learned to cook is because he didn't want to eat Grandma's hippie grub."

Phil laughed. "Mom prefers clean eating, which isn't always the tastiest."

Meg nudged her. "But she makes a mean lasagna."

As the talk about food continued, Aiden started to relax. The lasagna was delicious, the talk casual, and he began to feel like he belonged. The easy atmosphere changed with one shocked gasp from Mallory. The talk stopped and everyone looked at her.

"What is it?" Phil asked.

"Just a kick to the rib," she said breathlessly.

Phil didn't seem convinced, and neither was Aiden. Mallory had lost a few shades of color from her cheeks, and a hint of concern shaded her gray eyes. Aiden started to get up to check on her, but she darted her eyes across the table at Jessica.

"Hey, you know what I need?" Aiden asked. "Parmesan cheese. Jess, is there any in the fridge?"

"I'll check."

As soon as she was gone, Aiden said with a lowered voice, "What's wrong?"

"Nothing," Mal insisted. "Just a little discomfort. But I'm about to pop a baby in a month, so that's normal. Right?"

Meg leaned forward, pinning Mallory with a concerned gaze. "What kind of discomfort?"

Before she could answer, Jess returned and handed Aiden a bottle of pre-grated cheese. The tension around the table returned, but this time, it wasn't between Aiden and Meg. Phil continually glanced at Mallory, who had become unusually quiet. Meg did a good job of distracting Jessica, and their conversation filled the room. By the concerned look on Phil's face, Aiden guessed this wasn't the first time Mallory had had such severe "discomfort."

CHAPTER THREE

*M*eg left Mallory's the moment she could make an escape without being rude. She thought she'd done a pretty good job of hiding how eager she was to get away from Aiden. When Mallory started texting her just a few minutes after Meg arrived home, she used the opportunity to push Mallory to call Phil's mom. Kara was a midwife and would drop everything to check on Mallory.

As soon as Mal confirmed that Kara had arrived, Meg sank into a hot tub to try to wash thoughts of Aiden away. But she hadn't relaxed a bit. She kept replaying old memories of Aiden over and over in her mind. And then the recent one that was even more unnerving: his attempts at an apology. That night as she fell asleep, she was haunted by her conflicted feelings about Aiden past and Aiden present.

When she woke up after a restless night of bad dreams, she immediately texted to check on Mallory. And of course the very next thing she did was replay memories of Aiden breaking her heart. She battled her thoughts on the entire drive to work.

The morning passed in a fog of fatigue and frustration. She was struggling to concentrate on her work when Courtney, the office receptionist, poked her head into Meg's office.

"Hey," Courtney said with a tone of uncertainty. The usually perky woman bit her lip before whispering, "Aiden is here. He's asking for you."

Her first reaction was surprise. Why would he be there to see her? But she did her best to smile as if she were expecting him. "Thanks," she said as lightly as possible. If she let Courtney know how unsettled she was, that would only give everyone more to talk about. Instead, she walked into the lobby of the O'Connell Realty office as confidently as she would any other time. "I've got this," she announced, and like meerkats dropping back into their holes, the other agents disappeared into their offices. Even if they weren't watching, Meg suspected their ears would be tuned in.

"Mallory isn't here," she said to him. "Kara put her on bedrest until she can see her obstetrician."

"I know. I actually came to see you. If you aren't busy, do you think we could…"

He left the rest of his statement unspoken. She wanted to scream at him. He always did that. He always left things unsaid. and she'd finish his thoughts for him. He somehow thought that mattered. That he deserved credit for showing up and uttering just a few words. It didn't count. Unspoken words didn't count. Not anymore.

"What?" She refused to even consider budging until he said what he meant.

"Talk. About us. Where we go from here."

"Where we go?"

He shuffled his feet and stuffed his hand in his pockets. "I mean… how we make it easier to be around each other."

"I'm at work."

"Maybe I can steal you away for a coffee break?"

She wanted to refuse him. She *should* refuse him. However, if she didn't settle this now, she was never going to get anything done anyway. She'd replay him leaving and her broken heart and this conversation. She'd replay every moment she ever spent with him and every moment she spent missing him. The only way to break that insanity-inducing cycle before it started was to deal with him now.

She frowned, certain she was going to regret this. "Let me grab my things."

He smiled in response, and she wanted to retract her offer. He was getting his way. As always.

Meg reminded herself this wasn't about Aiden. This was about her. She was doing this to put the past to rest for herself. Not him. After gathering her coat and purse, she leaned into her boss's office. "I'll be back."

"Take your time," Marcus said.

She hadn't doubted the entire office knew the situation, but the paternal concern in his voice confirmed it. She'd seen that same look on his face when he was worried about Mallory, his wife, or his sister.

She didn't say anything to Aiden as they left the warmth of the office and marched toward her car.

Aiden matched her rushed stride. "A lot has changed since I left."

"Yes, I know."

"But the town still feels the same," he said once they were inside the car, "like nothing has changed at all. It's strange. Like living in some alternate universe."

She didn't respond. Nothing that came to her mind was nice. Maybe if he hadn't left, he would have been here when the café had been remodeled. Maybe if he hadn't left, he wouldn't feel so strange being here now. Maybe if he hadn't left, they would have made all their big dreams and out-of-reach goals a reality. Maybe she wouldn't have been too emotionally distraught to finish school and would have become a doctor like she'd planned.

She slammed her car door harder than was necessary and shoved the key into the ignition. The café was within walking distance, but she wasn't wearing the right shoes or the right attitude to go that far with Aiden at her side. She'd be too tempted to slip off her red Kenneth Cole bootie and shove the pointed heel through his eye.

He cleared his throat. "It's great that Mallory and Phil are having a baby, huh?"

Just like that, the sharp edge of her attitude softened, and she relaxed into a genuine smile for the first time since he'd suddenly appeared back in her life. Even Aiden couldn't diminish Meg's excitement about the baby. "Yes. It's wonderful."

"Do you know what they're having?"

"They want to be surprised," Meg said. "I can't imagine not knowing. It would drive me crazy."

Aiden laughed. "You always did have to plan ahead. You take Type A to the next level."

Her smile fell as she glanced over at him. He opened his mouth but didn't try to correct himself. She didn't correct him either, mostly because he was right. At least he used to be. He apparently hadn't realized the Meg of today was a different woman than the one he'd left behind. He claimed that he had changed over the last few years, but so had she. Apparently he didn't see that, but that didn't surprise her. Aiden always had preferred to live with his head shoved firmly up his ass.

She parked in front of Stonehill Café and climbed out, not bothering to wait for her passenger. Even so, he rushed around her to reach the door first, which he held open for her. She filled with dread once they were inside. Her attention settled on several familiar faces, and they all froze as Aiden moved to her side.

"Great," she whispered, knowing this would be the talk of their old social circles in no time. She looked at Aiden and was certain the same thought crossed his mind. He offered what could pass as a sympathetic smile.

Debbie Cooper finished muttering to her friends as she slid from the booth and rushed toward the former couple. "Oh, my," she cooed as innocently as a serial killer. "If it isn't *Doctor* Aiden Howard. How are you?"

"I'm good. You?"

"Just great. Hi, Megumi." She always said Meg's full name.

Meg hadn't determined if it was because her name was unique or because Debbie thought using her given name would remind Meg that she was Japanese. Meg figured it was the latter, but she didn't let it bother her. Debbie had dated one of Aiden's friends when they were in college, but she'd clearly been one of those women who treated the campus as husband hunting ground. She'd finished her degree and gone straight into professional child rearing.

Debbie grinned that beauty pageant grin of hers. "Well, I never thought I'd see you two together again. I mean, after the way you left, Aiden. Poor Megumi was devastated. We all were."

Meg scoffed at the blatant insincerity of the statement. "We're just having coffee, Debbie. Nothing to get excited about."

"Well, it's the perfect day for a hot cup of coffee."

"Sure is. Have a good day." Meg moved around the woman, dismissing her and her fake smiles. She dropped into a booth and let out a long breath. She didn't have to look in Debbie's direction to know the woman was keeping a close eye on what was happening at their table.

Aiden looked around before he finally seemed to work up the courage to speak. "I've wanted to apologize to you. For a long time. I just...I guess I was too much of a coward. But I am *so* sorry for the way I left. In my mind, I decided it was the best thing for both of us. You needed to finish med school, and I wanted to go forward with my residency."

"I'm going to call bullshit on that," Meg stated. She stopped when someone approached their table. "Hey, Jenna," she said to the café owner. "How are you feeling?"

The owner of the café touched her pregnant belly. "Like a punching bag. She's going crazy today. How are you?" Her question echoed with an edge in her tone.

Meg knew what she was really asking. Small-town news traveled fast. No doubt Jenna knew Aiden was Meg's ex.

"I'm okay," Meg said, answering the real question. "Can I get a coffee?"

"Sure thing. And for you?"

"Same," Aiden answered.

When they were alone, Meg continued. "We'd had a hundred conversations about our plans for the future, and not once did that include you ending things to move away. You blindsided me, and you did that intentionally. We had agreed on the list of places you were going to apply because they were close to schools where I could transfer. We had planned to make that move together, Aiden. You didn't even tell me you had applied to a residency in New York. You hid that from me. You lied to me about your intentions. Instead of just telling me you didn't want the life we had talked about, you bailed without warning. I should have seen it coming. I think on some level I did, but I'd convinced myself I was wrong about you. I wasn't."

He actually looked ashamed of himself, something she didn't know he knew how to do. "You're right. We did have plans. When we made them, I had every intention of following through. I got scared."

"I'm sure you did, but instead of talking to me about having doubts, you bailed."

"I know I hurt you. A lot. And I know you're angry."

They sat quietly as Jenna placed two mugs on the table. Once the woman moved to check on other customers, Meg pushed the sugar container closer to Aiden and watched him pour far too much into his mug. She'd never understood how he didn't have a cavity in every tooth with all the sugars he ate and drank. When they were together, she'd tried to get him to ease up on the sweets, but from the amount of sugar he'd added to his coffee, she guessed he never had.

She didn't want to think about their rare lazy mornings. On the occasions when their schedules synced up and they could be in the same place at the same time, they lazed around and sipped coffee and dreamed about the future they wanted. Meg had cherished—no, she had *lived* for those moments. She'd been such a fool.

"I thought you loved me," she said, surprised how weak her voice sounded.

"I did love you."

"No, Aiden, you couldn't have. You walked away. Like I didn't even matter to you."

He exhaled slowly. "I have been trying to find the courage to tell you, to explain."

"You don't have to explain. You aren't some puzzle that can't be solved. You were a cocky, self-centered asshole. You saw an out and you took it. You thought your life was just beginning and I was going to hold you back from something better. You thought you were going to go out into the world and life was going to be amazing and you'd never have to look back. But you got out there and realized it's ugly as hell, and all the sudden your little town and inexperienced girlfriend weren't so bad after all."

He stared at her. She waited for him to argue. He just kept staring.

"Am I wrong?" she finally asked.

"No."

She sipped her coffee and then looked around. Debbie was watching as she talked on the phone, and it took all Meg's strength not to flip her the bird. "You'd think she'd have better things to do than talk about us."

Aiden glanced in Debbie's direction but didn't let his attention linger. "Seeing us having coffee together is going to be good chatter for a while. But it'll pass."

"She loved it, you know? When you left. How you chose your career over me. She ate it up."

"You're right, Meg. I thought leaving everything—including you—was going to be the best thing. I thought I was going to go out and build some great life. Being in New York, seeing the things I did, was a not some great opportunity. It was a nightmare. You can't believe the shit I saw. It's insane what people do to each other. The kind of violence and neglect humans inflict on each other. It's crazy. But it was the wakeup call I needed to understand that I was lucky. I thought my life was so tough because my parents pushed me so hard and set rules and gave me expectations to live up to. I thought what you and I had was common, that I could find it again whenever I wanted it." He raked his hand over his hair and scoffed. "We loved each other, Meg. Really cared about each other. I didn't realize how rare that was."

Meg swallowed when the urge to wrap her arms around him and make him feel better hit her with the force of a jackhammer. He was clearly haunted by the things he'd been through during his residency. But she stopped herself from coddling him. That was her problem.

That had *always* been her problem. She was an enabler where Aiden was concerned. She'd always made excuses for his behavior and let him get away with everything.

Aiden had been too busy playing football with the guys to study for his chem test, so she'd stay up all night giving him a crash course. Aiden had spent his half of the rent on expensive clothes to impress his friends, so she'd rearranged her budget to cover him. Aiden had always needed rescuing, and Meg had always been on standby to save him.

She'd just been so happy to have someone who she finally felt was on her side, someone she'd thought she could be enough for, that she had waved off all his bad behaviors. She'd spent her life living in her sister's shadow, and Aiden had freed her from that self-imposed cage. She would have done anything to keep him.

She would have even dropped med school to move to New York. If only he'd given her the opportunity. She closed her eyes and sighed. "Can you answer one thing? Honestly?"

"I'll try."

"Why are you back? You were so determined to get out of here, even before breaking up with me. Why are you here, buying a house and taking a job at the hospital?"

He gave her a sad excuse for a smile. "Because I realized I was wrong. I made a mistake by leaving. I want to be here, with my family, which includes Phil and Mallory and their kids. And you. Even though you hate me."

"I don't hate you," she said. "I hate what you did. I hate the way you think. But I don't hate *you*." Despite her determination to hold on to her anger for the sake of self-preservation, she let go of some of the rage that had plagued her for the last four years. Seeing him struggling so hard to even look at her took some of the sting out of her suffering. She could never forget, but it was time to at least try to forgive.

"So," she said to break the awkward silence. "There's something else we need to talk about. I'm worried about Mallory. She needs to rest, whether she wants to or not."

"I agree," Aiden said.

"She doesn't need to be showing houses in her condition." She sighed heavily. "I'm going to push her to let me take over her clients so she doesn't overdo it."

Excitement lit in his eyes, as if he could read her mind and knew what was coming next. Damn him.

Swallowing hard, she forced the words out. "That includes you. If you're willing to—"

"I am," he said before she could finish. "Actually, I would love that. Not only to give Mallory a break, but..." He smiled uneasily. "You were right when you said we have to find a way to be comfortable around each other. This is perfect."

She didn't share his excitement but met his wavering smile. "Yeah. Perfect."

8h

Aiden hadn't expected Meg to help him find a new place, but he was glad she had offered. They'd left the coffee shop before whomever Debbie was calling could show up and witness the *Aiden and Meg Show.* Or at least that's what he imagined the gossipmongers would call it. He had, somewhere in his mind, known his sudden departure would be a source of gossip for their social group, but he hadn't allowed himself to think about how that might be like salt in her wounds. Part of him wished he'd said something to Debbie, but that would have only added to her list of things to talk about.

He wasn't exactly walking on air, but he was happy with how things were going since coming home, and he didn't want to mess that up by confronting someone who didn't even matter. Soon, he'd be starting his job at the hospital and on his way to buying a home. Doing so with Meg at his side would give him all the opportunity he needed to prove to her that he had grown up. He wasn't the spoiled kid he'd been when he left.

His good mood dimmed slightly when he walked into the kitchen and found his mother sitting at the table, staring at her laptop. Her slumped shoulders and downturned lips implied that she wasn't happy with whatever she was looking at. "Hey, Mom. What's up?"

She blinked a few times before closing the lid. "The only thing social media has accomplished is proving how stupid some people are."

"You'll get no argument from me." Grabbing a cookie from the container on the counter, he watched her cross her arms and lean back. He nearly laughed at the disapproving frown on her face. He hadn't seen that look in a long time. At least not directed at him. He suspected his younger brother still got it from time to time.

"My cousin is an idiot," she added without him prompting.

"Kara?"

"Yes, Kara."

Oh boy. He had begun to suspect getting his mom and her cousin on even ground was going to be harder than he had expected. Kara had left Stonehill when she was a pregnant teen and hadn't returned until a few years ago. Aiden's mother blamed her for tensions in the family, even though Kara left because her family had disowned her. Becca didn't think that was a good enough excuse for the strain Kara's disappearance had caused the family for more than twenty-five years and, clearly, caused even still.

"What'd she do now?" Aiden asked, taking a seat at the table.

Becca's frown deepened. "She's too old to have a toddler."

Aiden grinned. His mom was just a few years younger than Kara. Aiden couldn't imagine her with a young child, but the situation suited Kara perfectly. He didn't know the woman well, but he did know she was a midwife who took on underprivileged young mothers.

"She adopted a kid who was being neglected, Mom. How is that a bad thing?"

"There are plenty of other people in the world who could have taken Mira in. It didn't have to be Kara and Harry."

"Isn't that for them to decide?"

She narrowed her eyes at him, clearly frustrated that he wasn't seeing things her way. "All she does is mother pregnant teenagers and take care of babies."

Aiden finally heard the real issue through her angry words. Kara was the type of person who did what she wanted without worrying about what anyone thought. She was incredibly passionate about helping single mothers because she'd been one herself. She was passionate about art and learning new things. She kept busy helping others, another of her passions.

Becca had been a wonderful mother and homemaker, but Aiden couldn't really think of a single thing his mother was passionate about. She cared about her family, she volunteered at the school, but she wasn't *passionate*. Not like Kara.

He rested his cookie on a napkin. "You're right. She does have her hands full. Maybe you should offer her some help."

She scoffed. "If I asked Kara for help, she'd never let me live it down."

"You aren't asking *for* help. You are offering to help *her*."

Becca was considering it, he could tell, but she shook her head. "She wouldn't want my help."

Aiden was tempted to tell her she was being stubborn but decided to save his energy. As much as she complained about his father being narrowminded, Becca Howard could be just as guilty. Pushing her would only make her dig her feet in. Instead, he'd put the bug in Phil's ear to see if they could get Kara to extend the olive branch instead.

In the meantime, he was going to focus on finding a place to live. And mending his own fences—he'd made progress with Meg, but he still had a long way to go to earn her forgiveness.

CHAPTER FOUR

*A*iden arrived at Meg's office just before ten the next morning with two cups of coffee. He offered her one, which she accepted as she lifted a bright green faux leather bag onto her shoulder. That wouldn't have caught his attention, but it seemed to symbolize the change that had taken place in her after he left. His Meg had tended toward neutrals. She'd liked to blend in and go unnoticed. Post-Aiden Meg obviously preferred brighter colors. From the red ankle boots she'd worn the other day to the bright green bag, clearly she'd figured out how to express herself.

"Nice bag," he said when she caught him looking at it.

She slid her phone into the front pocket. "Thanks. It was a birthday gift from Aya."

He didn't miss the way she said her sister's name with a clipped tone. They were probably going at it again. He hadn't asked, but he knew enough about her family to guess they weren't happy about Meg being a real estate agent instead of a doctor. That was a subject he intended to broach at some point. Meg's family relations had always been tense, and he thought that probably hadn't changed.

"How is she doing?" he asked instead, keeping the talk of her sister neutral.

"Great. She's perfect." The sharp edge in her voice sharpened. "She's the lead molecular biologist on a team splitting DNA to make corn easier to grow in drought conditions. My parents are so proud of *her.*"

Aya had always strived to go as far above and beyond the bar their parents set that nothing Meg ever did seemed like enough. She always had resented her sister for that.

"Okay," she said breathlessly.

He wasn't sure if she'd worn herself out ranting about her sister or if she was emotionally bracing herself for spending the day with him. Either way, the exasperated sound twisted his heart.

"Ready?" she asked.

"Are *you* ready?"

"Ready as I'll ever be." She handed the receptionist a file folder. "This is where we'll be stopping today. I'll text along the way."

The woman behind the desk glanced at Aiden, her smile seemingly fixed in place. "Happy house hunting."

Meg stopped just outside the big glass front door and looked up at the sky. Big, fluffy snowflakes had started falling hard and fast early that morning. According to the forecast, snow would continue to accumulate until late afternoon.

A clump of wet, white fluff landed on her right eye and clung to her long lashes. She closed that eye and blew from the corner of her mouth. He couldn't stop himself from smiling as he watched the dislodged flakes float away. The moment brought back a memory from years ago: Meg bundled up and rushing from their apartment building toward his car. She'd been too intimidated to drive the short distance to campus in poor weather and had texted him, begging him to leave the library to pick her up. He couldn't believe his Meg had changed so much that driving in the elements didn't rattle her.

"Do you mind driving?" she asked. "One of the places I want to show you is a bit out of the way. I don't want us to get stuck in my car."

There it was. Meg may have changed, but some parts of the woman he'd known—the family angst and her fear of driving in bad weather—remained. That eased his mind in ways he couldn't begin to understand. He brushed aside his reaction to her and pulled his keys from his coat pocket. "Nope, that's fine."

As he climbed behind the steering wheel, she put her coffee into a cup holder and opened a file. Quiet fell between them after she rattled off the address of the first house they were going to view. He couldn't think of anything generic to talk about. Everything he could think to ask her was a reminder of the past, which would be a reminder that he'd walked out on her. He didn't want her to think about that. Not today. The lack of conversation wasn't exactly companionable silence, but at least he didn't have a rock in his gut and his heart wasn't racing with the anticipation of an argument.

Meg finally interrupted their quiet. "Number seven twenty-five. That's it. Right there."

"That's...nice." He examined the house through the windshield. The green siding certainly looked better in the photos. And the trees hadn't seemed so overgrown. "Quaint."

She chuckled. "Right."

They parked the car and carefully navigated the unshoveled walk. Meg pressed a code into the secure key holder dangling from the doorknob and then struggled to open the deadbolt lock. Finally, she was able to push the front door open and gestured for him to enter first.

Aiden winched as soon as he was inside. The house was straight out of the 1970s, complete with paneled walls and sunken living room. The only thing that seemed to be missing was a disco ball and platform shoes. "Wow."

Meg stopped beside him and scanned the living room. "Okay, let's look beyond the décor."

He ran a hand over the textured wallpaper. "Kind of hard to."

"You can change anything you don't like. Look at the layout and the structure. The bones. You're buying the bones."

"These bones?" He grabbed one of the wooden poles that lined an arched window. The window allowed viewing of the den from the small entryway, which was the starting point of dark green shag carpet that appeared to flow throughout.

"It's a bit of a fixer-upper," she said, "but it was at the bottom of your budget, so you will be able to make those changes. You liked the kitchen when we looked at pictures last night, remember? Let's check out the kitchen." She again gestured for him to lead.

They walked through the dining room to the kitchen—the only room that appeared to have been updated. This was the reason most of the pictures on the real estate agent's site had been of the new tile and appliances. He should have known the rest would be a disaster. Even with this house being on the low end of his budget, he couldn't afford to turn this into someplace he'd want to live. He'd have to gut it.

"Let's check out the basement." She opened one door, found the pantry, and then opened another that hid a set of stairs.

Aiden followed her down and opted not to mention the musty smell. She certainly smelled it too. The flooring at the bottom of the rickety old stairs was unfinished cement. It was dark. It was dingy. It was borderline frightening. The half-finished part of the basement had linoleum, a sofa, and haphazardly nailed-up green board in one corner of the room. The rest looked like it was ready for someone to come down and hack a body into pieces for easy disposal.

"Okay." She was obviously not impressed. "Let's look at house number two."

"You don't want to show me the yard? The bedrooms?" he teasingly asked.

"Honestly, I'm scared to see them. Let's just go. This house is not for you. Or any other decent human being."

"Agreed." He followed her upstairs, looking at his feet so he didn't watch something he shouldn't as she walked in front of him.

Back in his vehicle, she marked a huge X through the listing they'd just viewed and scribbled some notes on the page. "I don't think I'll show that to anyone else. Ever."

He laughed, and she read off the address for the next place. The silence between them returned, and he dared to ask the question that had been nagging him since his return. "When did you become a real estate agent?"

"About two years ago."

He clenched his jaw. Two years ago? She should have been finishing medical school two years ago. Asking about the past was likely to lead to a heated exchange, but he couldn't stop himself. "What about medical school? Didn't you finish?"

"No."

Glancing at her, expecting a more detailed answer, he scoffed as she continued focusing on the papers. "But you were so determined to become an obstetrician."

She didn't voice her frustration, but he could read her body language as easily now as he could four years ago. She lowered the papers, slowly turned her face toward him, and pinned him with her hard stare. "I was ready for a change."

"Why?"

Meg pressed her lips together. "Because. I was ready for a change."

Aiden wanted to press, but her glare was a good reminder that they were already walking a fine line. Starting an argument wouldn't accomplish anything at this point. The peace between them was as fragile as one of those sugar sculptures on the cooking shows she used to binge watch when she wasn't studying.

Their rare Sundays off had been her favorite days. He'd known that, still he'd often chosen to spend what should have been *their* afternoons with friends. She'd never complained, though. He'd disappear for a few hours and come back to their place to find her enjoying the quiet. Or at least that's what he'd told himself to appease his guilt. He'd given her time to enjoy the quiet.

Man, he really had been an ass. He had no idea why she'd tolerated him as long as she had. She should have been happy to see him go. Instead she'd stared at him as if she didn't understand the words coming from his mouth. Her eyes had filled with tears and her lip had trembled as she'd seemed to finally understand he was breaking up with her. Out of the blue. Without warning. And for no good reason.

The urge to apologize to her again sneaked up on him, but he stifled it as she rambled off information about the next house. Four bedrooms, two and a half baths, fenced yard, and, *oooh*, a hot tub. He was glad for the distraction.

She sorted through the pages a few more times before asking, "Why, uh, why three bedrooms?"

A few minutes ago, he wasn't willing to push her for answers, but if she got to ask questions, he figured he did as well. "You first," he pressed. "Why did you leave school?"

Meg stared at him. He waited, determined he wouldn't answer her question until she answered his. Turning her focus to the papers in her lap, she shuffled through several and then slammed the folder shut.

"I never wanted to go to medical school. That was my father's plan, not mine. I told you that a thousand times."

Back when they were dating, they'd curl up in bed and talk about the future. Aiden was so excited about becoming a doctor and thinking of all the good he was going to do in the world. Meg had never shared in his excitement. Finally, he'd nudged her to open up about why she didn't share his passion for medicine.

She hadn't decided what *she* wanted to do with her life. She said she'd never considered it because her life had been decided for her. She'd never had the courage to stand up to her father. He had started preparing her to be a doctor when she was a child. She got to choose her focus—obstetrics—but she had never felt like she got to choose her path. She'd been too scared to tell her father she didn't want to go into medicine.

Apparently that had changed. Aiden couldn't quite figure out what had led her to this job, though. The Meg he knew didn't have the personality for sales. She was quiet, a little meek at times. She was shy but brilliant and studious. Sales seemed to be the complete opposite of what she should be doing with her life.

"What did you father think about that?"

She laughed. "I'm sure you can imagine. Your turn. Why the big house, big yard, white picket fence?"

Aiden shrugged. "At some point, I hope to have a family. Not anytime soon, since I'm not even dating." He threw the last bit in for good measure. He had no expectation of them getting back together, but he could hope. He had to hope. So he wanted to make sure she knew he wasn't attached.

The smile she gave him didn't reach her eyes. They didn't reflect the excitement her upturned lips did. Her dark eyes looked surprised, maybe even a little hurt. "Oh. Good that you're thinking ahead."

It took a second to understand why she wasn't as impressed by his answer as he has been when he'd realized he should buy a bigger house. He'd patted himself on the back for considering the future when looking for a home. However, Meg was likely remembering how adamant he'd been that he didn't want children. He had wanted to focus on his career. He had wanted to travel and see the world. He had wanted material things, not a family.

"I needed time," he blurted out.

"What?"

Aiden tightened his hold on the steering wheel. There were a lot of things he wasn't ready to talk about, but he felt like he owed her some kind of reasoning on why he'd changed his mind. He knew he had hurt her with his past decisions, and he didn't want to do that again. "Being in New York, seeing the things I saw at the hospital there—it was what I needed to understand that I didn't want to live in that world. You know how I was. I had all those big dreams about how I was going to save so many lives and change the world. I was going to make a name for myself and have this grand life. It wasn't like that. It was just like you told me when I left. It was horrible, and I should have just stayed here and done my residency like we talked about."

She looked out the window at the passing houses. "You don't owe me an explanation."

"Actually, I do. That's the least I owe you."

She jerked her head around to glare at him. "Well, I don't want to hear it."

Aiden swallowed hard at the anger in her tone. "Meg—"

"You know, you should probably just work on home ownership first, Aiden. That's a pretty big commitment in and of itself. Maybe, *if* you can handle that, having a relationship with a human being won't seem so daunting." She closed her eyes and grunted out a frustrated sound. "*Goddamn it.* I was not going to lose my temper."

He blew out his breath slowly. "One step forward, five steps back, huh?"

"I'm sorry."

"Don't apologize. I deserved that."

She shook her head. "I don't want to be so bitter anymore. It just sneaks up on me."

He grinned. "It's good that you've learned how to release your anger instead of bottling it up. You used to just swallow it down and try to ignore it. This is a much healthier way to deal with your emotions."

"Turn right at the next block." Her words effectively ended the conversation. He had no right to discuss how she dealt with her emotions—then or now. She didn't have to say that. Her abrupt change of subject and hard tone did that for her.

He followed her instructions and pulled into the driveway. The two-story house looked like a photo out of a home improvement magazine. Though the landscaping was covered in snow, there were multiple bushes, and Aiden imagined they were complimented by flowers and plants of varying colors and sizes to present the perfect home. As they approached the porch, he smiled at how it was decorated for the holiday, with snowmen carved out of wood and strings of lights waiting to be plugged in, adding to the welcoming feel. The light yellow siding looked new against the crisp white window panes.

"I like this already," he said as Meg worked on releasing the key from the holder. "It's very homey."

She didn't respond. She simply unlocked the door and pushed it open for him to step inside. They slid their boots off, and then she guided him into a big living room. The house was a little older, so it didn't have the open concept that he'd been hoping for, but the vibe that rolled through him made this feel like home. The river stone fireplace needed a good scrubbing, but he could work with it—redo it, even. The flooring was manufactured wood but carried throughout and was obviously newer. The room was large enough that the big sofa in the middle didn't fill the space, and the row of tall windows along the front brought in lots of natural light. He liked this house.

"The kitchen's this way," Meg said.

He followed her to a room with long white countertops and a table tucked into a dining area. The appliances could be newer, but they were clean and worked. The bedrooms were good sized, and the bathrooms had been updated. When they stepped out the sliding glass door to the backyard, Aiden warmed despite the cold outside.

"This is great."

A tall privacy fence surrounded the yard. The cement patio had space for a grill and more than enough room for the family he didn't yet have. He tried to ignore the lack of enthusiasm Meg had as she talked about the newer roof and dry basement, but it stung him every time she lamely gestured into a room and spewed facts like a bored gameshow host. He felt something in this house. A sense of belonging or a hope for the future. He couldn't understand why she didn't feel it too.

As he wandered the upstairs, he could almost see his life here. A feeling akin to déjà vu found him. Not that he had been there *before* but that he would be there in the future. And as he stood in the master bedroom with Meg leaning against the doorjamb watching him, he had a sense that she belonged there with him.

The feeling was so strong and unexpected it nearly took his breath away. He wondered if she felt it too when she pushed herself upright.

"Take your time," she said dismissively. "I'll be downstairs when you're ready to look at the next one."

He wanted to stop her, but he didn't know what to say. He couldn't exactly ask her if she felt the same connection to the house that he did. How could he expect her to? Aiden toured the smaller bedrooms alone. The rooms would be perfect for the children he didn't even have.

Yet.

Before leaving, he returned to the living room to get a better look at the fireplace. Instead of focusing on the integrity of the structure, his attention fell on a photo of the family who lived there. A man and his wife sat with two children. Even though the photo was posed, their happiness was evident in their smiles.

Reality hit Aiden then. Everything fell into place. The real reason he'd returned home; the real reason he was so desperate to gain Meg's forgiveness. His failure to make a life in New York was so much more than the traumas he'd seen. His failure had begun the moment he left Meg standing in their apartment with tears on her cheeks and so much hurt in her eyes.

He finally understood the depth of his mistake—what he had really walked away from. He had known all along, in his arm's length way, that he'd lost the woman he loved and the future he had wanted with her. Standing here, in this house, looking at a photo that could have been them—should have been them—reality *finally* hit him. Like a kick to the gut.

The air in his lungs whooshed out of him, and he had to put his hand on the mantle to steady himself. All this time, he thought he just needed Meg's understanding and forgiveness so he could forgive himself. He needed more than that. He needed *her*. Their future. Their family. Their Sunday mornings reading the paper in bed, making love in the afternoon, ignoring the rest of the world until they absolutely couldn't anymore. Her laugher. He hadn't heard her laugh in years. He missed the musical sound that filtered in and warmed his heart. He wanted her back. He wanted their life back. A life he didn't deserve but suddenly understood that he couldn't continue without.

"Aiden?"

He turned his head when she called out to him. The look on her face and the tone of her voice let him know it wasn't the first time she'd said his name. He swallowed hard to resist the urge to pull her to him and hold her as he begged for another chance, begged her to believe in him again, and promised—*swore*—he'd never hurt her like he had before.

"Are you okay?" She started to reach out to him but stopped. "Do you need some water?"

Aiden had to fight to look away from her, but if he didn't, she was going to see right through him. He focused on the photo again. "Uh, no. No. I'm fine."

"You look like you could be sick."

"No. I'm good. I, uh, I didn't have breakfast."

She moved to his side and scanned his face, as though searching for signs of illness. "Oh. Well, let's get out of here and grab something to eat."

"Yeah, that sounds good. That sounds great, actually."

He glanced at the photo one more time. The happy family was like a sign from the universe that this was the house he needed to buy. This was his new home. The place where he would have the life he wanted. This was the place where he would win Meg back.

sh

"Feeling better?" Meg asked. She was unsettled by how quiet he'd been. Whenever Aiden was quiet, he was overthinking something. When he overthought things, he usually did something stupid. Like moving away without her.

He finished his hamburger and brushed his hands together. "Much."

"Good. So what did you think about the last place? You didn't say much."

"I liked it."

She smiled. She had suspected as much the moment they walked in. The house was perfect. Absolutely perfect. If Aiden didn't snatch it up, she might. She hadn't been looking for a home to buy, but that one was too good to let go. She had walked through the rooms and could actually imagine having a life there. "Great," she said. "Do you want to make an offer?"

"It's only the second place I've looked at. Let's check out the other place we picked out yesterday. It had a lot of potential."

She looked out the window, and anxiety settled in her gut. Even if she wasn't driving, she didn't like how the slush was starting to stick to the asphalt. The third house on their list was on the outskirts of town. "The snow is still coming down. If we are going to head out there, we should get going."

Aiden took a few of her fries and stuffed them in his mouth and then wiped his hands. He slid out of the booth and carried their tray to the trash can. Though Meg still felt nervous around him, she had relaxed quite a bit.

"So," he said after they climbed into his vehicle, "I haven't bought Phil and Mal anything for the baby yet, but I want to do something big."

She glanced at him, hating that he had surprised her once again. She wouldn't have guessed that Aiden even knew people gave baby gifts. "We already had a baby shower."

"But I wasn't there."

"Well, the baby's too little for beer and a foosball table, if that's what you're thinking."

He laughed. "I've outgrown that. *Kind of.* I mean, I'll still play if there's a table around, but I don't have one anymore. Of course," he said as he grinned, "that last basement was big enough for a foosball tourney."

She rolled her eyes dramatically. "Oh, you were terrible at that game."

"What? I was a champion. I bet Phil plays. I'm going to have to ask him about that."

He laughed and got a wistful look on his face, like he was imagining battling it out with his cousin while Mallory and... whatever woman he ended up with gossiped about whatever moms gossip about. The scene flashed through Meg's mind, and a strange pang, something far too close to envy, hit her.

"I was going to get a gift certificate to some fancy hotel with a restaurant so they can have a night off while I keep the baby," Aiden clarified, pulling her from her strange daydream.

A few moments passed before she fully understood what he'd said.

He had an idea for a baby gift. A really good idea for a baby gift. She stared at him, furrowing her brow.

His excitement seemed to dim. "Is that a terrible idea? I mean, I know they're not going to want to leave it—*him or her*—right way, but a gift certificate can be used anytime."

She frowned, disappointed she hadn't thought of that. "Actually, that's a really great idea. Kind of blows my portable crib out of the water, doesn't it?"

He grinned. "Well, I bring it up because...you know...I don't think that I should keep a baby all night by myself. Yeah, I'm a doctor, but I've never been a babysitter. So I was thinking maybe you could help me out with that?"

She rolled her eyes. "Oh. But you get all the credit, I suppose."

"Well, it was my idea."

"Mmm-hmm. Whose idea was it really?"

The shocked look on his face was as fake as his attempt to pass the idea off as his. "What? Like I can't be creative?" He laughed when she lifted a brow at him. "Okay, I looked up baby shower ideas online. I liked that one."

"Okay. You ante up half the money and half the babysitting. I'll do my half, and it's from both of us." As soon as she said that, she stuttered. Couples gave gifts "from both of us," not two individuals who were...whatever she and Aiden were.

"I can deal with that," he said, saving her from her straying thoughts.

They filled the drive with a debate about hotels and restaurants before paring down to two options they agreed to check out later—but not too much later since Mallory's due date was fast approaching. Meg practically squealed at the thought of holding the baby and confessed her plans to spoil the kid rotten. She couldn't stop herself from laughing. She even clapped her hands and bounced a little.

"He's going to be here before we know it. I can't wait." She glanced at him, and her smile fell. He was giving her the same look she figured she'd given him earlier—a complete *WTF* look. "What?"

"What?"

"Why are you looking at me like that?"

"I've missed your laugh," he said.

Her stomach twisted and her heart skipped. She had to turn away.

"Sorry," he said. "I didn't mean to make you uncomfortable."

"You didn't."

Actually, he had, but mostly because she couldn't pinpoint why her brain was going to such forbidden places. She decided to blame Mallory. Ever since she got married and started a family, Meg had this nagging in her heart. It felt like it was time for her to do the same. She wasn't even dating anyone! Why would she think about having a family? That was insane. But what was even crazier was that Aiden should fit in to that in any capacity.

"I'd really like it if we can be on an even keel," Meg blurted out. "Mallory was right when she said we have to put our past behind us so we can be there for the baby. I don't know what that means for us. I don't know if I want to be friends, or acquaintances, or...just two people who are nice to each other when we have to be. I do know that I don't want to keep hanging on to this anger. But I also know that I'll never be more than a friend. That's not going to happen, so if anywhere in your mind you are thinking we're going to get back together, forget it, okay?"

He looked at her, and she was certain she saw disappointment on his face, but he scoffed as if dismissing her statement. "All I said was I missed your laugh. Geez."

Aiden could deny it all he wanted, but Meg had seen through his façade. God. What did he think? He'd just strut back into town and she'd forget that he'd been a complete jerk? That he should have stayed a loner? That he didn't want *or* need her?

"There." She pointed as a house came into view.

He parked, and she hopped out before he could do something stupid like acknowledge that the air between them had grown tense again. She was opening the front door by the time he joined her.

"Nice," she said, looking around the contemporary styled house.

The walls were gray and the trim crisp and white. The open concept was something he had said he was looking for, but as he wandered through the big empty rooms, he seemed detached from the surroundings. The last house they'd looked at had brought out smiles and plans. He was quiet as he took in this space.

"Damn it," she said under her breath as she looked at him across the living room of the empty house. For a while she *had* forgotten that he'd done all those things. For a few moments today, things had felt normal between them. For a second or two, she had wanted things to be back to the way they were. She'd wanted him to want her back. She'd wanted to live in that house with him. With their children. She'd wanted the life he had promised her so long ago.

But the past was right there, reminding her that it was a bad idea to let him in. No, scratch that. It was a terrible, horrible, no-good idea, and she needed to forget it right now. Reminding him, and herself, that she wasn't going back down that road was her only defense, and she had jumped at it, but now she felt bad because she'd clearly hurt his feelings. He'd quieted down after her declaration.

"Well?" she asked, her question bouncing off the walls.

He slowly spun one more time before shaking his head. "I don't think so."

She wished he'd just make an offer on the last house they'd looked at and be done with it. He hadn't had a bad thing to say about it. He liked the colors, the kitchen, the finished basement, the fenced-in yard...everything. Even so, she asked, "Would you like to go back to the office and look at a few more listings?"

"Yeah, let's do that."

"Okay." She sighed and led him from toward the front door.

"You don't want to?" he asked as she locked the door and returned the key to the secure box.

With the key locked away, they headed for his vehicle. "You liked the last house. You're going to buy the last house. You know and I know it, so let's make an offer on it."

"I want to make sure it's the right one."

They climbed in, and she focused on latching her seat belt. "It's in the perfect location. The price is well within your budget. It had all the things on your list of wants. *And* I saw on your face that you wanted it. Stop being so wishy-washy and go for it."

As he started down the poorly paved road, he turned on the wipers to swipe away the huge snowflakes that just kept coming. "I'm not being wishy-washy. This is a big decision. I don't want to rush it."

She was about to push back when he hit a patch of ice, causing the SUV to slide toward the edge of the road. Aiden managed to keep his cool as he lost control. He didn't slam on the brake or jerk the wheel, but the vehicle just kept sliding. There were no guardrails between the road and the ditch—just a steep, snow-covered drop-off that looked increasingly dangerous as they approached it. Meg braced herself but was thrown forward and then bounced to the right. Her seat belt jerked, preventing her from going toward the dash, but she cried out when the side of her head cracked against the window.

It happened so quickly. Within a few heartbeats, the car slammed to a stop, nose first in the ditch, and Aiden put his hand to her arm. "Are you okay?"

She winced as she put her fingers to her forehead. The pain was sharp and intense, so much so that it took a moment for her to register the cut on the bone just above her eyebrow. "I think I'm bleeding."

"Look at me." He unhooked his seat belt and pushed her hand away. Holding her chin, he angled her head to get a better look at her injury. His panicked eyes skimmed over her brow. "You're going to need stitches in that."

"Great."

After jerking his scarf from around his neck, he balled it up and handed it to her. "Put some pressure on it."

"With your scarf?"

"Do you have something better?"

She put the material to her head and winced as she pressed against her wound.

"I've got a first aid kit in the back."

Meg widened her eyes and let her mouth gape open with shock. "You're going to give me stitches now?" she practically screamed.

The worry on his face eased into a slight smile. "No. But trust me, you're going to want an aspirin. Is it just your head? Is anything else hurt?"

"No, I'm good. You?" She hadn't even considered if he'd been hurt. "Are you okay?"

"Yeah. Sit tight."

He pushed the door opened and climbed out into the cold. While he walked around the back and released the hatch, she flipped the visor down and looked at her head. She thought she could get away with a butterfly stitch; however, the scar would be significantly less noticeable if the wound were stitched closed properly. Damn it.

"How bad is it out there?" she asked after he climbed back into the driver's seat.

"I don't think I can get us out of here."

She started digging for her phone. "I can make some calls."

"Let me look at that first. I may be able to push us out, but I want to bandage this before I do anything else."

Meg closed her eyes when he gently touched her face. Despite the coolness of his skin, heat rushed through her. She didn't want to react to him, but she couldn't help it. No matter what had happened, how much time had passed, her body remembered his touch and wanted more of it. That was dumb and dangerous.

He gently touched along her hairline. "Does that hurt?"

Meg appreciated the reminder that his touches weren't of a personal nature. "No."

"It's still bleeding pretty good. Put pressure on it again." Once she did, he said, "Open your eyes."

His voice was soft but so full of concern that Meg had to swallow hard to find the strength to do as he said. Why did he have to be so close? Why did she have to notice?

She cleared her throat and pulled away. "I'm fine, Aiden."

"You don't know that."

"I didn't hit that hard."

"You'd be surprised how little impact it takes to bruise a brain."

"Just because I didn't finish medical school doesn't mean I don't know how fragile the human body can be."

"I didn't mean it like that," he muttered.

He held up a penlight and flicked it back and forth, offering a distraction from his proximity. She couldn't see him as clearly, but she could still smell him, feel his hand on her, and feel small bursts of warm breath. Finally, he turned the light off and dug in his kit for something else. A moment later he asked her to lower the scarf. She did, and he touched her face again. Apparently satisfied that the bleeding had stopped, he applied a small butterfly bandage.

"There." He dropped his hands from her face. "That should hold until we can get you to the ER."

"The ER?"

"Don't argue with me on this," he said firmly. "You're not going to win." He pulled out a bottle and tapped two tablets into her hand.

She used her cold coffee to wash it down and winced. "Yuck."

Aiden set the first aid kit on the back seat and then put the gearshift into reverse. He gently pushed on the gas. The vehicle rocked slightly but didn't move more than a few inches. He tried again. And again.

"Okay, I'm going to have a better look and see if I can figure out how to get us out of here," he said. "Are you okay to wait, or should I call 9-1-1?"

She cocked her injured brow at him. She almost winced in pain, maybe did just a bit, but she refused to let him see how much that move had actually hurt. Instead, she climbed out and walked to the front of the car to have a look.

The front tire had gone over a huge branch that kept the treads several inches off the ground. No amount of pushing or accelerating was going to get them out of this mess.

"You were right," she said when Aiden came to stand beside her. "We're going to need a tow truck."

CHAPTER FIVE

"I really don't think this is necessary," Meg said. Again. Aiden wouldn't listen to her argument that she was fine with butterfly stitches. She knew how to care for her wound. She could take care of herself.

He ignored her as he continued examining her in the ER, once again flashing a penlight into her eyes. Then he tilted her head and pressed along the edge of the wound, causing her to jerk back.

"Leave it alone. The doctor will be here any minute. The *on-duty* doctor," she corrected when he glowered at her.

"Humor me, okay? I did this to you. I want to make sure you're okay."

She was about to argue that it had been an accident when the door opened and a woman walked in. The doctor was close to Aiden's age and just an inch or two shorter. When she saw him, she smiled widely, in a way that made it clear she was extremely happy to see him. Too happy, as far as Meg was concerned. Maybe this doctor was the reason he'd come back to town. He had said earlier that he wasn't dating anyone, but that would not be the first lie he'd ever told her.

Meg's stomach knotted, and she had the sudden urge to run.

"Doctor Howard," the other doctor said lightly, "I didn't expect to see you here until next week."

"I'm not on duty. The ice got the better of me unfortunately," he said. He gestured toward Meg. "My car slid off the road."

"Oh, no. Where at?"

"Out on old Johnson Road."

"My goodness. What in the world were you doing out there in this weather?"

Meg rolled her eyes as the woman carried on with Aiden like this were much more important than the gash in Meg's head. *Seriously?* Was this not the ER? Was she not sitting on the table with an open wound?

Aiden made a show of taking Meg's hand.

"We were looking at a place to buy out there," he said. "I think this was a good sign that we need to look in town. Don't you agree, honey?"

"Definitely," Meg said. She focused on the other woman. "I'd hate to have an accident like that once we have kids."

The woman forced her smile back in place. "Of course not. Let me take a look at your head. Oh, that looks painful."

"Oh," Meg returned with oozing sarcasm, "probably because it is." She had never been territorial before, but the frustration she felt at this woman flirting with Aiden right in front of her had instantly pissed her off. How freaking rude.

"Let's get some stitches in that and get you on your way." She looked at Aiden again. "I'm sure you'd rather not spend more time than necessary here. You'll be here plenty once you start."

Meg ground her teeth as the doctor stuck a needle in her forehead to numb the skin. She suspected the prick was delivered to be a bit more painful than was necessary, but she kept the accusation to herself. The stress radiating through the room didn't ease until the woman finished putting three stitches in Meg's forehead.

The doctor returned her attention to Aiden, asking if she needed to go over warning signs and symptoms that he should be on the lookout for. They laughed as he told her he thought he could handle it. Meg ground her teeth again.

The woman left with a flat smile.

As soon as the door closed, Meg scoffed. "Unbelievable."

Aiden leaned close and checked the doctor's work. "Looks good. Shouldn't leave much of a scar." Taking her hands, he helped her off the table. "Thank you."

"For what?"

"For not outing me as being a single doctor. I have a feeling that's a dangerous condition around here."

Meg scowled as her frustration grew a bit. "I didn't do it for *you*. What kind of doctor flirts when she has a patient on the table?"

"She was just being friendly."

"My ass." She sighed. "Can we go now? I'd really like to get home."

"No way. You need someone keeping an eye on you tonight. You're coming home with me."

"Oh, I bet your mother would *love* that."

He nodded, clearly realizing her sarcastic response was right on the money. His parents had always tolerated Meg but never seemed to care much for her. She'd never asked why, but she suspected having their sweet little *white* boy dating a Japanese girl had not made them happy. His mother always stuttered over saying Megumi but, much like Debbie, chose to use her full name instead of the shortened version most people used. Meg thought that was a way for people to remind her that she was different from most of the residents in Stonehill, as if she could somehow forget.

The small town had definitely gotten more diverse in recent years, but for a long time, the Tanaka family stood out amongst the *very* Caucasian crowd. Meg doubted either of Aiden's parents wanted him marrying or having a family with someone outside of that crowd.

"Okay. Call Mallory. I'll take you there."

"No. She'll be up all night checking on me. That's the last thing she needs this late in her pregnancy."

"Then I'm coming home with you."

Meg snorted. "I don't think so."

"You're not going home alone. If you have a concussion—"

"Stop it. I'm fine."

"Meg." He sighed as he dug his phone out of his pocket when it started ringing. "This isn't finished," he said before answering. "Hey, Phil. Meg's fine. We're just about to…" He trailed off as he listened, and then his eyes grew wide. "*Oh*. Oh, wow. Okay. We'll see you up in maternity, then."

Meg gasped as she grabbed his arm. "We're having a baby?"

He nodded.

"But she's early."

"Not enough to worry about," he assured her. "The baby will be okay."

"You're right." She exhaled a heavy breath. "You're absolutely right." She smiled and squealed loudly enough that a couple of nurses walking by looked their way. "We're having a baby!"

sh

Meg could tell Aiden she was fine a hundred times over—hell, she probably had—but he still didn't believe her. Logically, he knew she wasn't seriously injured, but that didn't make him worry less. Every time she shifted, sighed, or moaned, he sat up, ready to carry her downstairs to the emergency room if necessary.

She told him he was making her crazy, but he couldn't stop. Seeing the bruise forming on her brow, the swelling flesh surrounding the stitches holding her together, and knowing she was in pain, even though she refused to admit it, had him on edge. He wanted to hold her, comfort her, but she had made it clear she wanted him to back off. So he'd backed off. They sat on separate couches in the waiting room, and when Jessica came bouncing into the waiting room to tell the small gathering that she had a little brother, Aiden smiled awkwardly while Meg exchanged hugs with Mallory and Phil's family. Well, all of their family except him.

She insisted he could take her to her office to get her car, but he didn't want her to drive. And he insisted that she wasn't staying alone. Instead, he asked her for directions and drove her to her apartment.

By the time she opened the front door to her apartment, he could barely stand. They were both exhausted. He checked his watch and frowned at the late hour. Well, technically it was a very *early* hour. Almost two a.m.

He suspected if she weren't feeling as exhausted as him, she would have argued more about having him stay. The only other option he gave her was for him to call her sister. Someone had to stay with her. As he expected, Meg settled on him.

"It's chilly in here." He looked around for a moment before walking to the thermostat. He bumped the temperature up a few degrees and then turned to where he'd left her. She had fallen back onto the sofa and let her eyes close. Though he'd done so a hundred times, he leaned close to her and checked her stitches.

She didn't look at him, but she must have sensed him. "Do you think they're going to fall out or something?" she muttered.

He grinned. "The swelling is going down. Which is good since you didn't put ice on it like I kept reminding you to do."

"You're so bossy," she whispered.

"How about another aspirin before I put you to bed?"

"That would be amazing. In the medicine cabinet in the bathroom." She pointed to a door and closed her eyes.

In the bathroom, he opened the cabinet and chuckled aloud. When they had lived together, she had organized her medicine cabinet the exact same way. The bottles forward, alphabetically. She had changed in a lot of ways, but her need for organization was the same. He grabbed the first bottle on the top shelf and tapped out two pills.

"Don't go to sleep until you take these," he said, bypassing the sofa and heading into her kitchen. He went to the cabinet just right of the sink and opened it. Again, he smiled. If he opened the cabinet next to that, he suspected that would be where she put her bowls and plates. He peered in just to verify before he filled a glass halfway full of water.

When he joined her in the living room, she sat up and accepted the pills.

"Come on," he said as soon as she swallowed them down. "Let me put you to bed."

He followed as she led the way to her bedroom. The same framed image of "The Great Wave of Kanagawa" hung above her bed. The print had been given to her by her grandmother years ago and had meant the world to Meg. In all the time that he lived in New York City, he'd only made one trip to the Metropolitan Museum of Art.

He'd stood in front of the display of that image, thinking of Meg. He'd been mesmerized by the big blue and white wave, but not because of the beauty of the image. Because it reminded him of how foolish he'd been to leave the woman he had loved to chase a dream that had turned into a nightmare.

Standing there looking at the same print that he used to see every night before bed brought a strange sense of comfort to him. The same peace that being with Meg brought. The same comfort and familiarity he felt being with her.

"I can't believe how perfect the baby is," Meg said, falling onto her bed. "The most beautiful little boy ever."

Aiden covered her with blankets and smiled as he ran his fingertip down her nose before tapping the tip—something he hadn't done in four years yet was as familiar to him as breathing. She opened her eyes, wide with surprise, before he realized he shouldn't have done that. Their gazes locked, and his heart rolled in her chest. He hadn't meant to close the emotional distance between them, but the familiarity got the better of him. Pulling back, remembering that they were barely even friends now, he fisted his hand and shoved it in his pocket.

"I'm so sorry I broke your head," he said.

She stared, clearly surprised by his tender touch. "Yeah, me too."

"I'll be on the sofa if you need anything."

She grabbed his hand when he turned to walk away, startling him. He looked down at her, not sure what to expect. His heart swelled with a strange twisting of desire and dread. He couldn't deny that he still yearned for her or that his heart ached with the memories of a love he still couldn't let go.

"There are blankets and an extra pillow in the closet by the bathroom."

Aiden smiled his thanks and then left her to sleep. Grabbing the spare pillow and blanket, he stretched out on her couch and stared at the ceiling, telling himself that he'd blown his chance with Meg. No way was she going to give him a second chance, no matter how much he may have wanted it.

CHAPTER SIX

*T*his wasn't the first time Meg popped into Mallory's place after her exercise class, but this was the first time she felt weird about it. She parked next to Aiden's SUV, the front end still dented from their accident, and then looked at the black spandex pants she had worn. She had never been self-conscious about her dress before and wasn't at all above running into the store in sweatpants and a messy bun, but for some reason, having Aiden see her so unkempt didn't feel right.

"You used to live with the man," she reminded herself as she grabbed her purse and stomped up the sidewalk. He'd seen her in worse. Hell, he'd held her hair while she barfed after a few too many shots more than once. Spandex and a fitted T-shirt were nothing new.

Knocking, she bounced a little. The tight pants did little to ward off the chill of the December morning. She smiled at Phil when he opened the door. His dark hair stood in a dozen different directions, and his eyes were bloodshot.

"Oh, no. Was the baby up all night?"

He shook his head. "Not all night. I just couldn't get back to sleep. I haven't gotten back in the habit of sleeping when I can yet. Once I'm awake, I have a hard time drifting off again."

"How's Mallory?" she asked, slipping off her tennis shoes.

"I'm good," Mal said, coming out of the kitchen. She pouted and tilted her head as she watched Meg take her coat off. "I can't wait to go back to class with you."

"Soon," Meg said. "It's only been a week since you dropped a baby. Give it time." She tried to be casual about it, but she couldn't help glancing around and wondering where Aiden might be.

Mallory caught her scanning the room and smirked. "Aiden's gathering the trash to take out."

Meg forced a dismissive look to her face. "I was looking for Jess."

"She's at Mom's," Phil said.

"I want to hold this squishy little thing." Meg headed for Mallory and the little bundle she was holding. They had named their son Harrison Marcus after Phil's father and Mal's stepfather, but as of yet, they hadn't settled on what to actually call him. She snatched the bundle and cuddled the baby against her before kissing his little head. "You guys made such a cute human."

Mallory smiled. "We're going to call him Harris. We considered Squishy Little Thing and Cute Human, but they both seemed like a mouthful."

"Harris," Meg whispered, and even though she didn't think it was possible, she grew to love the little guy more. "I'm gonna be the best auntie you could ever ask for." Sitting in the rocking chair, she was stroking her finger over his cheek as he slept when Aiden came in.

"Got anything else..."

She smiled up at him. He was obviously surprised to see her, but she couldn't tell if this was a good or bad surprise. His mouth hung open as he stared before he blinked and snapped it shut.

"Uh, hey, Meg. I didn't hear you come in."

She smiled at him. "I'm stealthy like that."

He cleared his throat and continued on his mission. "Is that everything that needs to go out?"

"I think so," Phil answered. "Thanks so much."

"No problem." Aiden disappeared, and Meg returned her focus to the baby.

Within minutes Aiden had washed his hands and was closing in on her. "Were you out running?"

"I went to exercise class."

He leaned down and looked at the bruise and stitches on her head. "How did you feel during class?"

"Fine."

"Any headache or dizziness?"

"No, Dr. Howard."

"I wish you had consulted me first."

She flashed him an exaggerate scowl. "You're not my doctor."

Standing up, done looking at her head, he returned her scowl. "Did you consult *your* doctor first?"

Turning her face down to Harris, she whispered, "This is what is called overbearing and pushy. Don't ever put up with this."

"It's called being concerned," he countered. "I told Phil I'd make a grocery store run. Want to go?"

She was tempted to say no, but that was the exact reason she'd stopped by. She suspected if she left it up to Aiden, he'd get the wrong brands or flavors and Mallory would end up sending Phil anyway. The poor guy didn't look like he was going to make it through the day, let alone get to the store.

"This is where we part ways, little human nugget," she said to Harris. She kissed his head and started to stand. Aiden was quick to take her arm and help her up as if she couldn't manage it on her own.

She hated to admit it, but it was nice. And if they were a couple, she would have taken that as an indication of what a good husband and father would be someday in the future. But they weren't a couple. They'd tried that once and it had sucked. The relationship hadn't sucked. The ending had, and *that* had sucked bad enough that she wasn't going to go through it again.

"Thanks." She tried to say it casually, but it came out a little breathless. Mallory opened her arms, and the light that filled her eyes made a strange ache start in Meg's chest. She'd been adamant for the last few months that babies and husbands were not in her future plans, but something in her mind shifted in that moment. Okay. Maybe. Someday. Eventually… It might be nice to have this.

Easing Harris back into Mallory's arms, Meg couldn't resist putting a kiss on her best friend's head. "You're an amazing mama," she whispered. "Jessica and Harris are the luckiest kids in the world."

Mallory smiled up at her. "Thanks."

"Want me to start laundry or anything?"

"Nope. Mom and Marcus are coming over with dinner. She said she'd do a few loads then. Thank you for offering, though. I appreciate the help."

"Did you give Aiden a shopping list?"

"I did. Make sure he gets exactly what's on it. Please."

Meg winked. "I'm on it. You just sit there and be beautiful. We got this." She was slipping her feet back into her shoes when Aiden grabbed her coat and opened it for her. Damn it. He needed to stop being so nice and considerate. He was melting the sheet of ice she'd put around her heart, and that was making her feel vulnerable. She couldn't be vulnerable where he was concerned.

As she zipped her coat, he put his on and dug his keys out of the pocket.

"Oh, no." She held her keys up. "The last time you drove, I got stitches."

Aiden rolled his eyes, but he grinned and dropped his keys back into his pocket. She giggled as she opened the door.

sh

Aiden held up a box of cereal. "This?"

Meg shook her head and continued skimming the shelf. "This." She showed him the front, pointing to the little label that touted the box didn't contain any genetically modified ingredients. "Phil may try to snub his mother's hippie lifestyle, but she got to him more than he knows. GMOs are a big no-no in the Martinson-Canton diet."

Aiden grinned. "I guess there are worse things that someone could eliminate from their diet."

"Remember that guy in your chem class who ate so much garlic the scent literally seeped from his pores?"

Aiden pushed the cart as they moved down the snack aisle. He didn't want to think about how right this felt. Grocery shopping shouldn't make a calm wash over him, but he suspected it wasn't just the shopping. It was the normalcy of the morning. Seeing Meg nuzzling Harris. The way she'd whispered and smiled as she'd touched his face and kissed his head had sent an arrow right through his heart.

For a few seconds, he'd felt like he'd been dropped in an alternate world—a world where he hadn't been a chickenshit bastard who ran out on the life he should have had. Every time he thought he'd reconciled with his bad choices, something kicked him in the shins and he remembered.

If he hadn't left, he suspected that he and Meg wouldn't have lasted anyway. She clearly hadn't wanted the life she was setting herself up to have and wouldn't have changed course if Aiden had stayed. Had he stayed, he wouldn't have been broken down in the ways his residency in New York had humbled him. Things had unfolded like this for a reason. He accepted that. But then something as simple as seeing Meg smile would remind him that the only reason she wasn't with him was because he was a damned fool.

"Earth to Aiden," Meg sang.

He blinked a few times and shook his head. "Sorry. My mind wandered."

"You don't say." She stopped walking and narrowed her eyes a little. "Are you okay?"

"Yeah. You?"

"I'm good." She grinned. "What's going through your head?"

He couldn't tell her that he'd, once again, been thinking of how things could have been. Instead, he said, "We should stop and pick up that gift certificate we talked about getting for Mal and Phil. I don't want to forget."

She looked at the almond milk and non-dairy yogurt in the cart. "Probably should have done that first."

"Well, we can drop this off and then go back out." He liked that idea. A perfectly valid excuse to spend more time with her.

"Yeah, we could do that." She sounded doubtful.

"Unless you have somewhere else you need to be."

She thought for a moment before shaking her head. "No, that will work. I'm supposed to take Jessica to a movie today, and I haven't showered yet."

"Well. After we pick up the gift certificate, you can run home and shower while I go to Kara's to get Jessica. We'll swing by to pick you up, and then we can take her to the movie."

Meg stared at him. He'd probably just pushed a bit too hard. But then she smiled. "That'll work. Nice thinking, Doc."

Aiden smiled so wide his cheeks ached. "Of course, I guess that really depends on what movie you're seeing…"

Meg snorted. "Too late. You've already committed."

He let out a dramatic groan, but he didn't care what movie they saw. He didn't care if she and Jess picked out the cheesiest romantic comedy they could find playing in a theater. He was spending the day with Meg. That was all that mattered.

CHAPTER SEVEN

*A*iden was glad to be back in Stonehill for Christmas, but he had to admit he felt a bit disappointed by the holiday. When he was a kid, he waited all damn year to open presents. As an adult, it just wasn't the same. Stevie disappeared upstairs to play video games. His father was watching a football game, and his mother was flipping through a magazine.

"Phil and Mallory invited me over today. I bought a present for Jessica. Want to go with me?"

Becca looked at him and her eyes seemed excited for a moment, but then she shook her head. "No, thank you."

"Mom. Come with me."

"Kara wouldn't want me there."

"How do you know?"

She returned her attention to an ad that was apparently for jeans but more like soft pornography. "She didn't invite me."

"It's not her house. It's Phil's. Besides, I don't even know if Kara and Harry will be there."

"Well, Phil didn't invite me."

"He's got his hands full of dirty diapers and bottles at the moment."

"He invited you."

Aiden realized then how frustrating he must have been as a teenager. "Okay, Mom. Suit yourself." He started for the door but then stopped and faced her. "They're our family. Kara is our family. And it's Christmas Day. Maybe you could stop being mad at her for one day."

"I'm not mad at her," she snapped.

"If you say so."

"Aiden," she called. Slamming her magazine shut, she stood. "Wait."

She left him standing there for several minutes before returning with two gift bags. One had a baby on the front, and the other was clearly geared toward a teen. She grabbed one of the ever-ready tin of holiday cookies that she handed out to neighbors and surprise visitors during the holidays. "Okay," she said. "Let's go."

He decided to keep his sarcastic approval to himself. He guessed she had probably done that a hundred times or more as he grew up. He drove them to Phil's house, but as they got closer, she fidgeted, appearing more and more nervous.

Finally, he put his hand on hers to stop her from picking at her nails. "Mom. She's not going to body-slam you."

"I just don't want a fight. All we do is fight."

"Do you remember how Stevie and I used to get into it? We'd just pick and pick at each other until one of us blew up. Remember?"

"Yes. It was so foolish."

"You and Kara are grown-up versions of Stevie and me."

She opened her mouth as she looked at him but then snapped her jaw shut.

"You intentionally try to set each other off like it's a contest. So don't. Don't start with her, and if she starts with you, ignore it. Walk away. Don't engage." He parked on the street behind Harry's car.

"She's here," his mom said flatly.

"Don't. Engage."

After rolling her eyes at him, she climbed from his car and gathered the gifts. She waited for him to lead the way. She muttered something about this being a big mistake as the door opened. But as soon as she spotted the little bundle in Mallory's arms, she gasped and cooed.

Babies had that effect on his mother.

Mallory blinked with obvious surprise as Aiden stepped aside and let his mother go in first.

He lifted his hands. "Act casual," he whispered.

She chuckled and pulled back the blanket so Becca could get a better look at Harris.

"Oh, honey, he's perfect."

"Thanks, Becca."

Aiden led his mother into the house and put on a bright smile when Phil gave him the same "oh crap" look he'd gotten from Mallory. Kara stopped reading to her little girl to greet Aiden, and her eyes widened just a bit when she noticed Becca at his side.

"Hi, guys," Kara said, almost managing to cover her shock. She glanced toward the door. "Where's the rest of the crew?"

"Stevie's playing games, and Dad was watching football." Aiden put his arm around his mom's shoulders. "We're going to have to do."

Harry subtly nudged his wife, and she asked, "Did you have a good Christmas, Bec?"

"It's not over yet, Kare."

Kara opened her mouth, obviously ready to say something snarky, but Aiden gave her a pathetic look and she forced a smile. "Very true." Returning her attention to Mira, Kara started reading again.

Harry cleared his throat as he stood. "Here, Becca. Have a seat."

The tension between the cousins was obvious, apparently even to Mira, because she curled up closer to her mother.

"Nice," Phil whispered to Aiden.

"Let's just hope it takes."

"One step at a time."

"Hey, Aiden," Jessica said, running up to him. "Look at this!"

He skimmed the paper she showed him, but before he could fully grasp what it meant, she pulled it back.

"Mallory adopted me," Jessica announced proudly. "She's my mom now. Not just my stepmom but my real mom. Isn't that cool?"

He glanced at Mallory rocking the baby and smiling widely.

"We kept it under wraps because we thought Jessica should be the first to know," Phil explained.

"This was in my stocking this morning," Jess said. "It's the best Christmas ever." She leaned close and whispered, "I've always wanted a mom. Mine left when I was a baby and never came back."

"I'm really glad you got what you wanted, Jess." He held his hand up and let her give him a high-five. As soon as she did, she darted off to show Becca. Aiden guessed a lot of people were going to see that letter before Jessica's excitement wore off.

"That's awesome, Mal," he said.

She smiled even wider. "Thanks. We were really hoping to get it finalized *before* Harris was born, but we're very happy everything was legal before Christmas."

Looking around the room, from Mallory rocking Harris to Becca and Kara talking about raising kids, Aiden thought this was the most normal holiday he'd had in a very long time. He needed more of this. The only thing missing, besides his dad and brother, was Meg.

sh

Meg tried to ignore the way her sister was judging her, but the moment she had walked into her parents' house, Aya had lifted her chin at least two notches. However, when she focused on Meg's forehead, what appeared to be genuine concern filled her eyes. "How did that happen?"

Meg touched her still-tender injury. "I was showing some houses to a client. The roads were icy. We slid into a ditch."

"Meg," she said, as if she were already exhausted from dealing with her sister. "You know you shouldn't be driving in the snow. It scares you too much."

"I wasn't driving. He was."

Aya widened her eyes. "You got in a car with a stranger. A *male* stranger?"

"And here we go," Meg muttered. She'd literally been there for three minutes, and her sister was already getting ready to lecture her. If this were any other day, she'd snap to shut her up, but Meg was determined not to ruin Christmas. "All our clients have background checks, Aya."

"He could have killed you. Have you forgotten what happened to Annie O'Connell?"

"Her name is Annie Callison now," Meg said. "And since I work for her, I think it's safe to say I have not forgotten."

"She could have died."

"We have security in place to try to prevent anything like that from happening again."

Aya clearly wasn't impressed. She put her hands on the dining room table and glared. "This job is dangerous."

"So is yours. What happens if some spliced DNA gets into your system and you grow a third eye? Or turn into Spider-Man?"

"Stop being stupid," Aya snapped.

"You stop being paranoid."

"Your boss got shot, Meg. I'm not being paranoid."

"Peter Parker started shooting webs out of his hands."

Aya glared at her. Meg knew exactly how to get to her older sister, and she was doing it with a smile on her face. The downfall of being siblings was instinctively knowing how to piss the other off. Aya might be better than Meg at everything else, but she'd never outdo Meg in the area of deliberately pushing buttons.

"I'm trying to look out for you," Aya stated. "Someone has to since you obviously can't take care of yourself."

That zinger stung a bit more than Meg wanted to admit. "I do just fine, thank you."

"Not today," Umi said to both her daughters. "It's Christmas." She looked over her shoulder. "Stop before you upset your father. None of us need to deal with his bad mood."

Aya threw her hands up and left the room, headed toward the kitchen. Meg had intentionally arrived just in time to eat. She didn't want to deal with her sister telling her all the ways she was cooking wrong.

"Hey," Meg said before her mother scurried out too. "Why didn't you tell Aya about my accident?"

Her mother put her hand on her hip. Though she was small and thin, she looked intimidating as hell as she stared at Meg with her mouth stretched in a tight line and her eyes narrowed. "You really think I want your father to know you were with that boy?"

Meg blinked a few times. "You mean Aiden?"

"He's the reason you tossed your future away."

Rolling her head back, Meg moaned. "Seriously?"

"You dropped out of medical school because of him."

"No." Meg met her mom's determined stare with one of her own. "I dropped out of med school because I didn't want to be a doctor."

"Not today, Megumi. Don't start this fight today."

Snapping her mouth shut, she exhaled. She shouldn't have told her mom that she'd been with Aiden. That was stupid, and she'd known it before she'd even said it. She had just been feeling so confused about him, and Mallory was busy with the new baby. She'd needed someone to talk to and had foolishly thought she could tell her mother. Her family couldn't possibly understand. She knew better.

Dropping into a chair, she waited for her mom and sister to finish bringing food from the kitchen. As they served, Meg's father joined them, barely acknowledging Meg. Aya, on the other hand, was quizzed about the trials and tribulations of DNA splicing. She wasn't dating, had no plans to, but she was ready to move out of her apartment and buy a condo. She'd looked at a few already but hadn't found one she liked.

"What?" Meg blurted out. "Why would you..." She looked at her mother as if she could somehow help her make sense of what she'd heard. "Aya, why would you let someone else show you condos? You could have come to me."

"I went to a professional real estate agent, Meg," Aya said.

Ouch. "Um. I've been a licensed agent for over two years now. I think most people would consider that being a professional."

"He has over *twenty* years' experience," she said, as if that justified choosing someone else over her sister. "This is a serious decision for me, Meg. I have to go with an agent I can trust."

Meg sat back, her mouth open and her eyes wide. "Oh. Gotcha. Someone you can *trust*." She looked at her plate of half-eaten food and her stomach clenched. Letting her breath out slowly, she pushed down the angry words trying to escape her. *Not today*, her mom had told her. *Not today.*

"Not today," she whispered as she stood. "Excuse me. I just realized I'm supposed to be somewhere else."

"Sit," her mom said. "Megumi. Sit."

"Merry Christmas, Mom," she said and headed for the door.

Meg left without looking back. She wasn't lying; she did have other places to be, but Mallory and Phil weren't expecting her for another hour or two. She swallowed down her emotions, refusing to let Aya's choices hurt her, giving herself a much-needed pep talk the entire way.

However, when she noticed Aiden's car parked outside, what was left of her spirits sank. Damn it. She didn't need this. She didn't need to see him. Not now. She considered driving by, but she had been invited to celebrate with her friends—who were more like family. And she did need to be with them right now. Aiden be damned.

However, she hadn't expected to see his mother sitting next to Kara. Becca Howard had never been a big fan of Meg's. She didn't know why, but she had her suspicions. Aiden's parents were old-fashioned, and Meg didn't have to consider for very long that they didn't approve of their son dating a girl from Japan.

Meg and Aiden had dated for two years, and she had only seen his parents a handful of times. His family preferred to make excuses for why they couldn't spend time with Aiden and Meg rather than getting to know her. She imagined his mother probably breathed a huge sigh of relief when Aiden moved to New York to get away from Meg.

When she looked up and caught Meg's gaze, she seemed just as surprised. Her eyes immediately darted to Aiden, who didn't see the exchange because he was crossing the room to Meg. She frowned at him. He never seemed to have caught on to the fact that his mother didn't approve of their relationship.

"I wasn't expecting to see you today," he said.

"Ditto," she muttered as she tugged her coat free.

He pulled it from her and hung it on the wall. The look he gave her was sympathetic curiosity. They might not be together anymore, but she knew that look. He always gave her that after she returned from visiting her parents. They had a way of draining her light, and Aiden had a way of seeing how dim she felt afterward.

In the old days, he would have scooped her up and cuddled her in his lap, giving her reassurances while she vented and ranted and eventually cried. Then he'd order dinner in and they'd snuggle in a pile of blankets and watch television while her soul recuperated.

Damn it, she needed that now. She needed him to hold her close and promise her that she would be okay. She needed him to whisper that she was enough and she would always be enough. But then she remembered that she wasn't. If she had been enough for him, he never would have left her.

Turning away from him and the reminder of the pain he'd caused, she focused on the only other person in the world who could mend her broken heart. She opened her arms as Jessica came running up to her.

"Look at this," Jessica said.

Meg took the letter and had to hold her breath to stop herself from sobbing. She'd known that Mallory planned to adopt Jessica, but she didn't know it was finalized. She wasn't surprised they'd kept it a secret, and rightfully so. Jessica should have been the first to know.

"This is amazing," Meg said.

Jessica's smile fell a bit. "Are you upset?"

Meg sniffed and shook her head hard. "I'm happy, kiddo. That's so exciting."

The smile returned to Jess's face. "I get to call her Mom now," she whispered.

Pulling her close, Meg hugged Jessica and kissed the top of her head. Of all the times she needed a little boost from the perpetually happy kid, this was it. Her Christmas had been as bad as expected, and she felt gutted from the little time she'd spent with her family. Holding Jessica close, she whispered, "And she'll be the best mom in the whole world. You're so lucky."

"What's wrong, Meg?" Jessica asked.

"Hey," Aiden said, far more cheerfully than the moment called for, "did you open the present I brought for you?"

Jessica hesitated but then rushed to where Aiden had set the wrapped boxes on the table. Meg shook her head at him. She didn't want to talk about it but wasn't surprised when he took her hand and pulled her toward the kitchen.

"What happened?" he asked softly.

"The usual."

"Megumi," he stated firmly. "What happened?"

She pointed to her head, to the stitches still holding her healing skin together. "I let it slip that you were the client I was with when this happened. My parents freaked out. My sister gloated. I got mad. We all blew up. And then I stormed out. So...the usual."

He creased his brow. "Why would they care if you were with me?"

She scoffed. "Just...because. I was surprised to see your mom here." She smiled when his eyes lit, not only because she'd managed to distract him but because it was nice to see him excited.

"She and Kara are being civil. That's a nice change."

Meg smiled. "Christmas miracle."

He shoved his hands in his pockets. "Not the only one. Look at us acting like friends."

She was startled by his observation, but once the shock faded, she felt warmth touch her heart. "Nice, huh?"

"Very nice. I'm sorry you had a bad Christmas. I hope it gets better now that you're here."

"It will."

Mallory eased the kitchen door open and poked her head in. "Aiden, would you go help Phil...do something in the other room please?"

He hesitated before leaving through the door Mal held open for him. As soon as Mallory gave Meg a sad, understanding smile, Meg felt her depression returning.

"I mentioned Aiden was back in town. My sister freaked."

"I'm sorry."

She shrugged. "Well. My entire family blames him for me falling into such a deep depression that I couldn't finish medical school."

Mal pressed her lips together. "You did fall into such a deep depression that you couldn't finish medical school."

"Not because of Aiden." She sighed when Mallory simply stared. "Not *only* because of Aiden. Depression is a little more complex than one bad relationship. Okay?"

"I know that, Meg," she whispered. "I was there, remember?"

Meg held her breath. "You didn't tell Aiden I was diagnosed with depression, did you?"

"No," Mallory stated firmly. "I would never share your private business, Meg. But maybe you should tell him."

"It's none of his business."

She bit her lips. "Did you ever tell your parents about your diagnosis?"

"It's not theirs either," Meg insisted.

"Maybe they would be a bit more forgiving if they knew it wasn't just a bad breakup that sent you spiraling."

Meg shook her head. Her family would never understand. They already thought she was a failure. Adding that she battled depression to her long list of faults would only make things worse. She knew Mallory didn't agree with keeping secrets, but the only person who knew the depth of Meg's struggles was her best friend. Mallory had been the one to notice the signs and helped Meg get treatment. The bond between them only grew stronger after that, whereas Meg's bond with her family became more strained.

They would never understand. She knew that as well as she knew that if she told Aiden how far she fell after he left, he'd feel guilty. It wasn't his fault. She'd been ill. She'd needed help. She'd gotten it. End of story. Nobody else needed to know.

"I'm starving," Meg said, intentionally changing the subject. "When do we eat?"

CHAPTER EIGHT

*A*iden was probably pushing his luck, but he couldn't help himself. His first shift at the hospital had been amazing. Not only did he not treat a single malnourished or obviously abused child, but he'd even had time to rest. The ER in Stonehill was nothing like New York, where the patients outnumbered the doctors ten to one most of the time. Aiden was able to actually treat a patient before he was needed again. It was amazing.

That on the heels of what he would call an incredibly successful Christmas made him feel like he was invincible. So invincible, in fact, that he decided to drop into Meg's office and invite her out for a celebratory lunch. He was sure she'd join him. They'd texted a few times, had a few phone calls, and he was feeling really good about the progress they'd made. She wouldn't turn him down. He was certain.

He smiled at the O'Connell Realty receptionist who picked up the phone and called Meg before he even asked.

"Go on back," she said.

He gave her his most winning smile, but she didn't seem impressed. She raised her brows and focused on her computer screen.

Aiden almost laughed. He certainly had a reputation with her coworkers, and not a good one. "Good afternoon, Miss Tanaka," he said.

She leaned back and furrowed her brow. "Did we have an appointment?"

"No."

"Then why are you here?"

"I don't want to eat lunch alone. That would dampen the amazing mood I'm in. Tell me you're free."

Suspicion touched her eyes, but then she chuckled. That was a look he hadn't gotten from her for a long time, and it lifted his spirits even more.

Sitting across from her, he said, "Are you free for lunch?"

"Maybe. Where are you going?"

"Wherever you want."

"Are you buying?"

He put his hand to his heart. "Oh. You are a tough negotiator. No wonder I got such a good deal on that house. Yeah. I'm buying. Come on."

"Sweet," she sang out as she jumped up. "Let's go to the café."

He scrunched his nose. "Jenna always looks at me like she's going to spit in my food."

Meg laughed as she put her coat on. "That's because I told her to."

"I'm not kidding."

"Neither am I." She smiled at him, and his heart lifted. "How about that Italian place on the square?"

"The café is fine." He followed her from the office and opened the passenger door for her. Though they rode to the restaurant in silence, it was comfortable, lacking the stress they'd shared just a week or so before. Gauging her easy attitude, he dared to put his hand to the small of her back as he opened the door to guide her in. She didn't call him on it. In fact, he thought he saw her grin a little. They slid into a booth, and he sat back. "Tell me about your Christmas."

She shook her head, and he was taken aback by the sadness in her eyes.

"Hey," he pressed, suddenly concerned. "You have to talk to me about this, Meg. What happened?"

"I do *not* have to talk to you about it. I talked to Mallory, and I'm fine."

"Okay. I *need* you to talk to me about it. What happened?"

She hesitated and then shrugged. "The usual 'Meg's a loser' talk."

"You're not a loser."

"Well, I'm not a doctor."

Aiden waited for the sarcastic smirk on her face to fall. "You're an amazing real estate agent. You're smart and funny. Kind of cute sometimes too."

She grinned a little. "Shut up."

Reaching across the table, he took her hand. "I'm sorry you didn't have a good holiday. But you have to remember that this is your life. Not theirs. You have to do what makes you happy."

She nodded but didn't seem convinced. When Jenna approached the table, they ordered drinks and then took a minute to review the menu. By the time Jenna returned with two teas, they were ready to place their lunch orders.

"Are you happy?" Aiden asked when Jenna left their table. "With your job, I mean?"

"I love my job."

"So what they think doesn't matter. I know it sucks that they don't support you. But at the end of the day, Meg, it doesn't matter what they want. Your life is not theirs. Your happiness is not theirs. It's yours."

"I know that, Aiden. But it still sucks to know they are so disappointed in me."

"I'm not disappointed in you. In fact, I'm proud as hell of you."

She creased her brow.

"When we were together, you were not the person you are now. The woman you are today is fun and relaxed and real. You used to be so stressed out and terrified of failure that you could barely breathe. I could be wrong, but I'm guessing this change in you is because you gave up trying to be the person your parents wanted you to be."

She frowned. "You're not wrong. As soon as I gave up trying to live up to their expectations, I felt like I could breathe for the first time. But I also lost my family."

"You didn't."

"I did. Aiden, I can't be the person they want me to be, and they can't accept that I don't want to be. My father thinks it's a deliberate insult to him. He thinks I dropped out of medical school to embarrass him."

"And what do your mom and Aya think?"

She snorted. "Aya loves it because she's the perfect daughter now. Who knows what Mom thinks. She just wants me to keep my head down and not make waves."

"That's the exact opposite of what you should do."

She looked at him. "What do you mean?"

"Are you ever going to go back to medical school?"

"Hell no."

"So you need to explain that, Meg. You need to tell him this is who you are. You are his daughter. And he has to accept that you aren't going to be what he wants you to be. He has to accept that you are *you*."

"Fat chance," she muttered. "But thank you. Really. Thank you for trying to help. How was your Christmas?"

"Really good, actually. Mom and Kara didn't kill each other, so I consider that a win."

Meg smiled. "I'm glad. So you and Phil are one step closer to uniting the Martinson-Canton-Howard clan."

"I think so."

"Congratulations." She toasted him with her tea, and he happily clinked his glass to hers.

"Thank you."

"Megumi?"

They both looked at who had called her name. Aiden might have forgotten her sister's name, but he hadn't forgotten her face. She stood, staring, her eyes wide and mouth hanging open.

"What are you doing with *him*?" she demanded.

Meg laughed a strained and borderline maniacal laugh. Aiden knew this confrontation was not going to end well.

sh

Meg stared at her sister with disbelief. Who the hell did she think she was? Oh, no. Meg knew exactly who she thought she was. Setting her glass down, she said, "Excuse me," to Aiden and slid from the booth. Standing eye-to-eye with Aya, she glared. "Let's take this outside."

Aya snorted. "Like a Western."

"Like nobody needs to hear what I have to say to you."

"Meg." Aiden's voice was a soft but firm warning. He used that tone on the rare occasion that she'd lose her temper with him. It was his way of trying to ease her back before she jumped into a pit of her own boiling anger.

She lifted her hand to quiet him.

"Stay out of this, asshole," Aya said to him.

"Hey," Meg snapped. "You don't talk to my clients that way. Oh," she said sarcastically when Aya widened her eyes with surprise. "You probably didn't realize this, but I don't just play real estate agent. I actually get clients and buy and sell houses."

The confusion on Aya's face didn't ease. "This guy ruined your life."

"No. This guy *saved* my life."

"By breaking your heart so bad you had to drop out of school?"

Meg shook her head. "How many times do I have to tell you that had nothing to do with Aiden?"

"Oh, you just so happened to throw away your future around the same time he dumped you?"

"Ladies," Jenna said, "How are we doing?"

Meg pressed her lips together. "Sorry, Jen. We're leaving." As she grabbed her coat and bag, she gave Aiden an apologetic half smile. Ignoring the stares of other diners, she marched toward the door with Aya at her side. The moment they were outside, she turned. "I cannot believe you just made a scene like that."

"*Me?*" Aya shrieked.

"You have no right confronting me about my life choices."

"I'm your sister."

"Which apparently means jack shit to you, Aya. You deliberately chose to use a different real estate agent just to spite me. Don't even try to deny it." Tears poked at the back of her eyes, and she had to clench her teeth together to stop them from forming. "You did that to hurt me."

Aya creased her forehead. "I did not."

"Oh, right. You just wanted a *professional*."

Straightening her back and jutting her chin out in that way she did, Aya glared but then shook her head. "That has nothing to do with you having lunch with that jerk. What are you doing, Meg? He broke your heart."

"That was a long time ago."

"He hurt you," Aya said softly.

"You hurt me all the time," Meg stated.

Aya blinked, clearly surprised. "What?"

"You absolutely love that our parents think I'm a failure. You absolutely love pointing out how you think you're so much smarter and better you are. You're not, Aya. Do you know why you're not? Because you're miserable."

"I am not."

"Really... Do you remember how you wanted to be a painter? You wanted to take art lessons, but you weren't allowed. Remember?"

"I was a kid. I grew out of that."

"No, you let Dad push you into a mold you didn't want to be in. You used to watch that annoying Bob Ross show for hours and try to teach yourself. Remember? You wanted that so much that you tried to teach yourself because Dad wouldn't let you take lessons. I remember because you used to ask me to help you, and I was so proud of you for doing what you wanted, despite what he said. But then you gave up. All you did was study to get into the college he said you needed to get into to have the career he said you had to have."

Aya seemed a bit stung by Meg's assessment, but she shook it off. "And look where I am now. I'm a lead scientist. I'm highly respected in my field. People look up to me."

"I'm highly respected in my field too. My coworkers adore me. I have really good friends now. They love and protect me. You think you're the first one to come to my defense where Aiden is concerned, Aya? I didn't drop out of medical school because Aiden left. I *woke up* because Aiden left. He was the only thing that made medical school bearable. I was able to convince myself that I was doing it for us—for Aiden and me—and not for Dad. I could pretend that I wanted to be a doctor because that's what Aiden wanted. Once he was gone and I was staring down a future I didn't want, I realized I couldn't do it. I didn't want to do it."

Aya stared hard at her sister. "You broke their hearts."

"I didn't want that, but maybe they should have let me decide my future for myself."

"You're a salesperson, Meg."

She nodded. "Yeah. And a damn good one. But you know what else? I'm happy, Aya. I'm *really* happy. Are you?"

Aya's cold exterior showed the first real signs of cracking when a tear slid down her cheek. She swiped it away and looked around the square.

"I know Mom and Dad don't understand," Meg said. "But I thought you would. You're my sister. If anyone knows how hard it is to live up to their expectations, it should be you."

"They expect a lot from us because they want us to be successful."

"I am successful. I have a job I love, friends I love, and I'm living on my own. They don't support me—financially or emotionally," she added. "Everything I've accomplished has been from my hard work."

"You live in a dinky apartment."

Meg lifted her brows. "Yeah. Because I'm saving for a house, Aya."

"Your car is a dinky old sedan."

Meg pointed. "Well you've also got the debt that went with buying your fancy car. My car is paid off, and my rent is a fraction of my income. Do you honestly think that just because I haven't buried myself in debt, I'm not successful? Let me explain something that being a real estate agent has pounded into my head. Being upside down in debt is not a symbol of success."

"I'm not upside down in debt, Meg. I have things because I have a job that allows me to afford them."

"Are you sure? I think you have those things because Dad convinced you that you need them to prove to others that you're successful. The Aya I remember wanted a bright red motorcycle and a house on the beach of the Outer Banks."

Aya got that sad look in her eyes again. "I was a kid, Meg."

"Yeah. A happy one."

"If I recall, you wanted to be a baker or something. You didn't do that any more than I became an artist."

Meg reached into her purse and pulled out her phone. She opened the gallery of photos and swiped until she found one of her and a group of her friends wearing chef hats and showing off their creations. "I didn't become a baker, but I attend baking classes every week." She swiped a few more pictures and showed her another. "And I take art classes." She laughed slightly. "Once a month we have painting parties with wine and lots of laughing."

Aya smiled but still looked broken. "Do you do landscapes?"

"Of course. I mean"—she shrugged—"they look like a drunk penguin painted them, but I do it."

Finally, Aya laughed. but then her face crumpled and tears filled her eyes. "You always were the brave one, Meg. I could never do that."

"Yes, you could, Aya. You just have to stop listening to Dad's voice in your head. It's okay to try and not be perfect. Sometimes messing up is the fun part."

Wiping her cheeks, Aya glanced at the café. "Is that why you're having lunch with him? Because messing up is fun?"

"Aiden broke my heart, Aya. I loved him so much, and then he just left."

"I remember."

"But we were kids back then. Neither one of us had grown up yet. We're not back together, but I think we're becoming friends again."

"You're okay with that?"

She nodded. "My best friend is married to his cousin. So I have to be okay with that because we are going to see a lot of each other."

"But you're helping him buy a house? Why would you put yourself through that?"

"Because the only way to deal with the hurt is to face it. I've been avoiding facing the hurt you and our parents have caused me, but this"—she gestured between them—"has made me realize that it's time to face that pain too. I know you are all disappointed in me for dropping out of medical school, but that was a long time ago and you need to get over it. I'm living the life I want to live, and that's my right. You're my family and I love you, but if you can't accept that this is who I am, and love me anyway, then maybe I don't need to be around you guys anymore. What you did at Christmas dinner, Aya, telling me that you hired a professional instead of me, was like a knife to my heart. I'm really tired of you acting like I'm something to be mocked and laughed at. I made my own choices, and they were the right choices for me. I'm sorry you can't respect that, but I will no longer tolerate being talked down to. If that means that I don't see you anymore, then that's the way it has to be."

Aya sniffed and shook her head. "I'm sorry, Meg. I'm so sorry." Aya wasn't a hugger, but she hugged Meg then, tight and unrelenting. "I'm jealous, okay? I'm so jealous of you that I can't breathe sometimes." Finally, she pulled back. "Look at you. You're so smart and pretty. People like you."

"People like you. A little," Meg added and giggled through her tears.

"I didn't know how to stand up to Dad back then. I still don't. You always did what you wanted and didn't care that he got mad."

"I cared. I just couldn't be what he wanted. I was so unhappy. Aiden leaving was the best thing that ever happened to me." She didn't realize how true that was until she said the words. "It crushed me, and when I bounced back, I bounced back a million times stronger and more determined to be who I wanted to be."

"So, I just need to find some jackass to break my heart?" Aya asked.

"Maybe."

"I'm glad to hear that you're happy," Aya whispered. "And I really am sorry I hurt you."

"I forgive you."

Aya glanced toward the café again. "Be careful with him, Meg."

"I am. We're just friends."

"I know how much you loved him."

"Yes. But do you know how much I love you?" she asked in a teasing voice.

"Don't," Aya begged with a moan.

Too late. Meg took her hand and dramatically started belting out an old pop song they used to dance to behind their closed bedroom door. Dressed up in heels and far too dark makeup, they'd pretend to be superstars like Celine Dion and Mariah Carey. Aya eventually laughed, but it took until the second verse.

Meg smiled and stopped singing. "Are we okay?"

"You tell me. I'm the one who was a jerk."

"We're okay," Meg said. "Would you like to join us for lunch? Please," she begged when Aya bit her lip.

"I called him an asshole."

"You weren't wrong," Meg said and laughed. "He's changed, Aya."

"You say that with far too much affection."

"Sit with us. Take a minute to see that we've grown up."

Aya nodded. "On one condition."

"What?"

"You take me to one of your painting parties."

Meg smiled wide. "Deal."

CHAPTER NINE

Meg didn't want to think about how close Aiden was to her, but as he carefully clipped the stitches in her head, she could feel his breath tickling her cheek. Why did he have to *freaking* breathe? Closing her eyes, she forced out her own breath.

"Does this hurt?" he asked, sounding concerned.

"No."

"You're going to feel a little tug."

As he pulled the threads from her skin, she had to admit he'd turned out to be an amazing doctor. She hadn't expected that. Then again, the fact that he was removing her stitches in Mallory's guest bathroom was probably not the best reference for his medical skills. Of course, he'd pointed out, if she'd made an appointment with her doctor like he'd been telling her, he wouldn't have had to do this himself.

"That's so cool," Jessica whispered with awe. Looking at Aiden, she asked, "Can people with Down syndrome be doctors?"

"People with Down syndrome can be anything they want," Meg

said before Aiden could offer his own answer. Encouraging Jessica was a requirement as far as Meg was concerned. The girl had enough struggles in her life without people shooting down her dreams.

"As long as you work hard and pass all your tests," Aiden added.

"Do I have to do math? Math is hard."

"Math is hard," Aiden agreed. "Meg had to help me a lot with math when we were in school."

"Meg is smart," Jessica stated, not leaving room for debate.

Meg smiled and offered the girl a wink.

"That's it," Aiden said. "Stitches are out. Several days later than they should have been."

"Save the lecture for someone who will listen, Doc," Meg said.

"I'm going to go ask Mom if I can go to doctor school," Jessica announced and ran from the room.

Meg smiled as she left them. "Poor Phil is like chopped liver ever since Mallory adopted her. She never wants to talk to him about things anymore."

Aiden chuckled as he washed the little scissors and tweezers he'd used for his mini-operation. "How are you and Aya doing?"

"We seem to be able to tolerate each other right now. It won't last, but it's nice for now. Thank you again for being nice enough to accept her apology at the café the other day."

He looked at her. "Your family has every right to be angry at me for what happened between us."

"Yeah, but her lashing out wasn't about you."

Leaning his hip against the sink as he dried his hands, he offered her a sweet smile. Damn it. He was far too good at those sweet smiles lately. "I'm glad you two are working things out. I hope that extends to your parents at some point."

"I'm sure it will, but I can only fix one broken relationship at a time."

"Oh, so if you're working on your relationship with Aya right now, does that mean we're fixed?"

She blew a sarcastic raspberry. "That's so last season, Aiden."

"Good. I'd like to start the new year knowing we're better."

"We're better," she said sincerely.

The smile on his face spread and lit his eyes. "Good."

"How are your mom and Kara getting along?"

He chuckled and gave his head a hard shake. "Um. Depends on the day. She's going to start helping Kara out a few hours a week. I guess Kara has a hard time with her daughter's separation anxiety."

"Yeah, that kid's always been like glue to her mom."

"She seemed to take to my mom okay, so they are hoping they can start working on putting some time and space between them so Mira can overcome her clinginess."

"Well, she had a tough life before they adopted her, so I don't think anyone can blame her for having codependency issues."

"I agree, but I'm glad to see them working on them now." He hung up the towel, but instead of leaving the bathroom, he resumed his stance against the sink. "Things like that can become increasingly difficult to resolve with age."

"Are you a shrink now too?" she teased.

He shrugged. "In my downtime."

Meg grinned.

"Would you two like me to bring some drinks and snacks in here?" Mallory asked from the door, Harris strapped to her chest in the soft blue wrap Kara had made for her. "Or do you plan to rejoin the party soon?"

"I'll have a beer and a slice of pizza," Meg said.

"That's cute. Except there isn't any pizza because you two were supposed to order it and pick it up before Dr. Howard decided to turn my bathroom into a triage center."

"Actually, a triage center—"

"*Pizza*," Mallory stated. "Now, please. People are starving."

"Now," Meg mimicked with a whisper as soon as Mallory disappeared.

Aiden took her hand and pulled her with him from the bathroom and down the hall. Aiden pulled his keys from his pocket, but Meg grabbed them.

"Oh, no," she said, holding up her keys. "When you drive, I get stitches."

He rolled his eyes but laughed as he followed her out of the house.

sh

The small gathering around Aiden started *quietly* counting down to midnight. Jessica was spending the night with Mallory's parents, but Harris was sound asleep in his crib just down the hall. They all intended to keep him that way. Aiden looked around the room, and his throat tightened with an unexpected surge of emotion. He was bringing in the new year surrounded by his cousin and the new set of friends he was making. And Meg.

He thought they were really making progress. She didn't seem to harbor the anger and resentment anymore, and he no longer felt the need to apologize for the past every time he saw her. They had started spending a lot of time hanging out with Mallory and Phil, helping with the baby and running errands for the new parents. They had even taken Jessica to a movie to give Phil and Mallory time alone while Harris napped. The easy relationship he had made with Phil and

Mallory was more than Aiden had hoped for when initially reconnecting with his cousin. The fact that Mallory and Meg were already close friends had just been the icing on the cake.

The four of them were falling into a routine that felt so natural, Aiden couldn't help but hope that this was what his life was going to continue to be even after Harris was bigger and his parents weren't so exhausted from caring for a newborn. Aiden still hoped that Sunday afternoons were spent with Meg. Maybe not doing laundry and running to the store for Mallory and Phil, but maybe for themselves. Relaxing days off like they used to have.

The irony wasn't lost on him that fearing a future like that was what had led him to run away from Meg in the first place. Back then, the normalcy of housekeeping and grocery shopping seemed like a curse. Now, it seemed like everything.

As the countdown to the new year reached one, Aiden was tempted to lean down and kiss Meg as the rest of the couples in the room were doing. But they weren't a couple, and he was clearly reminded of that when she simply pecked a kiss on his cheek. "Happy New Year, Aiden."

He pulled her closer and held her a bit tighter than he should have. "Happy New Year, Megumi." This was the first time he'd rung in the New Year with her in a long time. Even though he refused to let it be the last, he was going to cherish this moment.

When she pulled back from him, she gave him a warning glare, but the smile on her face showed she was teasing. Aiden wished the night didn't have to end, but soon people started moving toward the door.

Meg finished gathering dirty dishes, despite Mallory's insistence that she would clean up in the morning. Aiden helped, mostly because he wasn't ready to leave Meg's side just yet. That was silly, he knew, but the ringing in of a new year had him filled with the stereotypical hope that so many had on the first of January. He carried a stack of empty pizza boxes through the kitchen door and out into the cold to stuff them in the already-full recycling bin. There had only been about a dozen or so people there, but they had certainly gone through the food and beer during their celebration.

Rushing back in to get out of the cold, Aiden stopped in his tracks when he saw Meg putting on her coat to leave. The evening they hadn't technically spent together was coming to an end, and disappointment filled his chest.

Meg spotted him and flashed a smile. "Drive home safe, Aiden."

"You too," he said as casually as he could. He wanted to tell her to wait on him, that he'd walk her out, but she had her sister with her. No need to make them all feel awkward.

When she was gone, he turned to the kitchen where Mallory and Phil were filling the dishwasher. Or at least they had been. Now, Mallory was standing with her hand on her hip with her lips pressed together and Phil had his arms crossed, leaning against the counter and smirking.

"What?" Aiden asked.

"What?" Phil repeated.

Aiden lifted his hands. "What?"

Phil scoffed. "Dude, you are so obvious."

"Do people still say dude?" Aiden asked Mallory.

"He just did," she said flatly.

"What's the problem?" he asked.

Mallory shook her finger at him. "You listen to me, Aiden. Family or not, I'll rip your face off if you hurt Meg again."

Oh. Shoving his hands in his pockets, he let out a long sigh. "Listen, I'm pretty sure Meg has no desire for us to be more than friends. But if, by some miracle, she did give me a second chance, I wouldn't be stupid enough to blow it. I lost her once. If I had her back, I'd never let her go again."

Mallory softened her stance. "You better not. I just had a baby. I don't want to go to prison."

CHAPTER TEN

*A*dmitting that her anger had subsided seemed to ease the tension Meg felt around Aiden. New Year's Eve had been the most fun she'd had in a long time, and though the regret of not kissing him at midnight had lingered in the back of her mind, she managed to ignore it...most of the time. Even better than she and Aiden moving on from the past was that Meg and Aya were actually acting like sisters instead of mortal enemies. They hadn't been so close and easy around each other for years.

Meg felt like so many of the relationships in her life had mended, and that was easing stressors she hadn't even realized were weighing her down. Of course, she still had a long way to go with her parents, but she wasn't confident those were relationships that would ever be fully mended. She had spent too many nights lately tossing and turning, trying to find a way to make them understand she wasn't a failure just because she didn't have M.D. after her name. She was going to have to confront her father at some point, but for now, she was content just to accept that she had made peace with her ex-boyfriend and her sister.

The front door opened, and Meg's heart fluttered a little as she glanced at the clock on her computer screen and confirmed the time. That should be her ex-boyfriend right now. Grabbing the folder with his name on it, she set the stack of papers on the opposite side of her desk and grabbed a pen.

"Hey there," he said, walking in.

She smiled. "You ready for this?"

He rubbed his hands together and blew out a breath. "Ready as I'll ever be, I guess." Taking the seat across from her, he stared at the stack of papers. "This is crazy," he said, but the smile on his face wasn't one of fear. He was so excited, and she was excited for him.

Meg chuckled. "Yeah. Quite the commitment you're making here." She grinned when he glared at her playfully and then snatched the pen she held out to him. "I've tagged all the places you need to sign and initial."

He flipped through the pages, legally taking ownership of the home that had crept into her dreams more than once over the last few weeks. She chose not to analyze why her subconscious had continually put her in that home with Aiden. Just because she decided to give up the anger and bitterness that had hounded her for years didn't mean they were going to go back to the way things were.

They had a good thing going here. They had become friends. The time they spent helping out Mallory and Phil had somehow become a regular thing, but eventually they weren't going to need as much support as Aiden and Meg were giving them. Mallory and Phil had already resumed their own grocery shopping. Instead of roaming up and down aisles, Aiden and Meg had started sitting around their living room, but they couldn't do that forever. With their parents rolling through to see them and the kids, they likely weren't getting as much privacy as they needed. Eventually, Meg and Aiden would have to stop dropping in every Saturday afternoon to occupy their sofa.

Aiden turned to the last page and huffed out a big breath, pulling Meg's attention back to him.

"Okay." He glanced up at her and smiled. "This is it."

As soon as he scribbled his name on the last line, she slid a ring full of various keys across the desk to him. "Congratulations. You are a homeowner. The previous owners labeled the keys. There are a few copies of front door keys, and the others—well, you can test them all out when you get there."

He laughed as he picked up the keys while she gathered the papers. "Are you ready?" he asked.

Meg stopped moving. "Ready for what?"

He looked at her like the answer was the most obvious thing ever. "To go check out my new place."

Her heart did a little flip in her chest. "Uh, this is usually the end of the line for the agent. You're on your own now."

"Come on." He stood. "You know you want to come over."

"No." She chuckled. "I don't." She said the words, but as soon as they left her mouth, she realized they weren't true. She did want to go over. She wanted to walk in and feel that rush of knowing that was her home. But it wasn't her home. It was Aiden's home, and she had no place there. The urge, however, made her realize that she was probably ready to get serious about looking for her first house. She'd saved enough for a down payment on a home she could call her own. It was time to start taking the same steps toward being a responsible, full-grown adult that Aiden was taking.

"Come on," he pleaded. "Don't make me do this alone. This is a big milestone for me. I want to share it with someone."

The plea in his voice tugged at her heart, but she shook her head, refusing to let it pull her in. "Call your mother."

"I can't. She and Kara took Mira to the children's museum today."

Meg lifted her brows in surprise. "Together?"

"Together."

"Wow. I'm impressed."

"Don't be. At least not until they come home and we can verify they made it out alive."

Meg giggled. Everything seemed to be falling into place for him. She was a little bit jealous if she were to admit it. She had to guess that was because he was being assertive, taking control, and making things happen. That had never been something Meg had been good at. She was usually pushed along. First, she let her parents dictate a future she didn't want, and when the pressure became too much and she cracked, she fell into the habit of letting Mallory push her along.

That had actually turned out to be a good thing. Mallory's insight and awareness had led Meg to getting the treatment she needed to battle the dark clouds that had always plagued her. With the right medication, she had finally been able to blossom on her own. But that didn't mean she was good at plugging along like Aiden was doing. She tended to find a comfortable place and stay there until she no longer could.

If Mallory hadn't moved to California after graduation, Meg never would have had her own place. A place she still lived in, even though Mallory had come home and gotten married and started a life of her own. Meg was still in the same spot she'd been when Mallory left her.

She needed a kick in the pants. Maybe this would be it. "Okay," she conceded. "I don't usually do this with clients, but I'll go with you. Give me just a minute." She busied herself with stuffing the papers in an envelope to be dealt with later and grabbed her purse from her desk drawer. She turned to leave with him and then stopped at the sight of him sliding a key from the jumbled keychain. He held one out to her. "Wh-What's that for?"

"For the front door."

Her heart did that funny little flipping thing again. He was giving her a key to his house? That seemed like...a commitment to something that they hadn't committed to. "I know that, but why do I need a key to your house?"

He shrugged. "Somebody has to feed the dog I haven't yet bought when I go on a vacation I haven't yet scheduled."

She moved around him. "That's why you have Phil."

"I'll get him one too, but this one is for you."

Meg didn't take the key, but it clinked as he set it on her desk. He clearly didn't intend to take no for an answer. The last time he'd given her a key to his place, it was like signing a death warrant on their relationship. They didn't even have a relationship now, but she still felt the same sense of doom wash over her as she had felt four years ago. The first signs of commitment coming from Aiden Howard had been the first signs of the end.

Her mouth went dry as she tried to dismiss the feeling. "You should change the locks, Aiden. The previous owners may have kept a copy or have given a spare set to someone out there. You don't know who might have access to your house. Change the locks before you move in, okay?"

He nodded and grabbed his key back. "Okay. I'll give you one for the new locks."

She didn't respond as she led him out of her office. "I'll be back soon," she told Courtney.

The woman didn't say it, but Meg was pretty sure she was thinking that Meg had been sucked into Aiden Howard's trap again.

The feeling began overshadowing the good she'd felt just an hour ago. Up until he'd tried to give her access to his home, she had been confident they'd made huge strides in their relationship. Him giving her a key shouldn't have taken so much wind out of her sails, but damned if it hadn't.

They'd lived together for just under a year before he left her. They'd had everything so well planned out.

"Are you okay?" Aiden asked after several minutes of intense silence.

"Yeah."

"Meg?" he pressed.

She looked out the window. "I like where we are right now, Aiden. We're friends. I like that."

"Me too."

"I don't think trying to be more than that would be a good idea."

He didn't answer, and she didn't know what else to say. They rode in silence until he parked in front of his new house. Meg's heart grew inexplicably heavy as she examined the structure. Neither made a move to get out of the car when he cut the engine.

He tapped his fingers on the steering wheel a few times. "I love you, Meg," he blurted out.

Her heart dropped as she jerked her face toward him. She knew her eyes were wide and her mouth gaping from his unexpected words, but she couldn't control her reaction. Of all the things she expected to hear from him, that was probably the last. When he'd left her years ago, he'd tried to tell her that he loved her, but she hadn't believed him. How could he possibly leave if he loved her?

"Don't lie," she whispered before he could say more.

"I'm not."

"Aiden."

He was quiet for a moment before continuing. "I've always loved you. I wasn't ready to love you, but I did. I thought of you every day when I was gone. I wanted to call you so many times—"

"*Aiden.*"

"It's the truth, Meg. I'm not going to push for more because I'm the one who blew it, but I want you to know that I never stopped loving you." He climbed from the SUV then and started for the house.

She hesitated before she followed him inside. All the furnishings and photos had been removed, but it still felt like she belonged here as she looked around the living room. She had felt that the first time she'd walked into this house. She remembered thinking that if Aiden didn't make an offer on this house, she would. She felt at home here in a way she'd never felt walking into any other house. She'd shown hundreds of homes, but this was the only one that had ever resonated with her.

Something about this house made her want to be here. She wanted to be cooking in that kitchen and relaxing by the fire in this living room. She wanted to belong here. In this home. In *Aiden's* home.

Damn it. She'd be stupid to let herself fall for him again. She'd be setting herself up for a fall. But looking at him, she believed he had changed. He had grown. So had she. There were many things about them that were the same, but they were different people now. They were the people they had been too afraid to be four years ago. They were who they were meant to be, and they still fit. When she blocked out what her brain was telling her and listened to her heart, they still felt right to her.

This felt right to her.

Aiden stopped moving around the empty house and stopped in front of her. "So what do you think?"

She creased her brow. "What?"

He grinned, but it wasn't as easy and natural as it had been before his confession. "I knew you weren't listening. Did you hear anything I said?"

"Sorry." She dismissed her overwhelming emotions with a laugh. "I…"

Aiden's teasing smile fell. "I shouldn't have said that in the car. We're in a good place, and I should have left well enough alone. I'm sorry."

"No. No. I just…" She looked away from him as her heart screamed at her. *Listen to me*, it begged. Meg bit her lip and looked out the window at the big back yard where he said he wanted to let his dog roam and his future kids play. "I love you too," she said before her mind interfered. However, her brain couldn't let her stop there, so it quickly added, "But I don't trust you. And I don't know how to."

He looked hurt by her words but not surprised. "I don't blame you. I hurt you, probably more than I could ever fully understand." A sheen covered his eyes, but he blinked it away and cleared his throat. "Do you think…" Clearing his throat a second time, he looked at her, staring intently in her eyes. "Will you let me try to earn your trust again?"

Holding her breath, she debated what to say. She wanted that. She hadn't even realized how much she wanted that.

"I just want to try, Meg."

Biting her lip, she let her heart and brain battle it out. Finally, she whispered. "I'll think about it."

He nodded. "Okay." Turning away from her, he tried to lighten the mood around them by gesturing around the empty space. "In the meantime, I need someone to help me decorate. I'm terrible at that. What do you say? Shall we talk paint colors?"

Meg wanted that. She wanted to be excited about decorating this house, but she suspected taking a step back was the most logical thing to do right now. "You know, you should ask Mal. She's great at this kind of thing."

Aiden looked like he wanted to press, but he nodded instead. "Okay. But when she picks a color you don't like, I don't want to hear it."

She forced a laugh. "I'll bite my tongue."

"So furniture shopping is out, then?" He winked as he teased her.

sh

Aiden dangled his keys as he walked into his mom's kitchen. "Look what I got today."

Her face lit with a proud smile. "Congratulations. I'm so happy for you."

"Thanks. Dinner smells good."

"Chicken cordon bleu."

"Yum."

She wiped her hands on a towel and reached for plates to set out. "How was the museum?"

Becca let out a long breath. "That cousin of mine has the patience of a saint with that kid. Mira wouldn't even play with the other kids. Kara had to do everything with her."

"Well, my understanding is Mira has been pretty tightly bound to Kara since birth."

Becca sat at the island. "It's sad, really. I didn't know the entire story until today. That girl's birth mother was a disaster. Who knows what would have happened to that baby if Kara and Harry hadn't taken her in."

Aiden smiled. For the first time ever, his mother sounded like she approved of something her cousin had done.

"I can understand why Mira doesn't want to let Kara out of her sight," she said, "but if she doesn't break that kid of her separation anxiety now, they're going to have real problems as she gets older."

"Well, isn't that part of what today was? Trying to get Mira to get comfortable doing things without her mom?"

Becca nodded as a thoughtful look fell over her face. "I think if I start spending more time with her, I'll be able to help. Eventually she'll feel more comfortable around me, and maybe she'll let someone other than Harry step in when Kara isn't around."

"That'd be really good, Mom. I know they could really use some help especially now that Phil and Mallory have a newborn. They used to distract Mira quite a bit."

"Oh, yes, they won't be able to help now that Harris is here. I'm sure Kara needs more help than she's willing to admit."

Though she did slip a dig in at her cousin, Aiden was happy to see a sense of purpose in her eyes. She sat a bit taller as she seemed to let the realization that she was needed sink in.

"So, you own a house now," his mom said. "When will you be moving in?"

"I'd like to paint first. But I don't even know what colors."

Her eyes lit even brighter. "Want help?"

He did, but he had been hoping Meg would want that job. Since she didn't, at least he could help his mom feel needed. "Yeah. That'd be great. Thanks. I think I also want to update the fireplace. Meg gave me the name of a contractor that should be able to help."

One of her brows lifted. "Meg. You mean..."

"Megumi Tanaka. She was my real estate agent. I thought I told you that."

"Uh. No. I mean, I knew you went with O'Connell Realty, but I guess I assumed Mallory helped you."

"Mallory was far too pregnant to show me houses." He sensed his mom was put out by the news that Meg had helped him. He was about to call her on it, but Stevie walked into the kitchen. "Hey, little bro. What's up?"

"When do we eat?" Stevie asked in true growing teenaged boy fashion.

Fully distracted, their mother went to the stove and started lecturing Stevie. Apparently he'd left his shoes in the entryway just waiting for someone to trip over them. Instead of listening to that, Aiden pulled his phone out of his pocket and texted his cousin, asking if he would be willing to take time soon to help him paint.

CHAPTER ELEVEN

*A*iden had never been so happy to see his mother as he was when she walked in with three large pizzas the next night. "Dinner," he called out, his voice echoing around the house.

His mom smiled as she took in the almond color he'd added to the walls earlier in the day. Meg had stared at the wall as he covered the previous paint with the fresh. She hadn't said it, but he suspected she thought the color was too boring and safe. And he hadn't pointed out that she had passed on the opportunity to choose the colors in his new home. He hadn't wanted to add more thing to Mallory's plate, so he'd asked his mom, who had jumped at the chance.

Becca Howard had played it safe, as she tended to do. The wildest color in the house would be the light green she'd chosen for the bathrooms. She'd chosen that color because she'd bought a shower curtain that his father hated and wouldn't let her hang so she gave it to Aiden instead. His bathrooms were painted based on a secondhand shower curtain. He kissed his mother's head because it was so classically Becca Howard. He couldn't do anything but chuckle.

"This looks great, honey," she said as he took the pizzas from her.

"Do I smell pepperoni?" Meg asked, walking into the room with splatters of light green on her hands and face. She stopped and her smile froze. "Hi, Becca."

His mother froze too. "Me-*Meguma*," she said in her usual stuttering way. She had always tripped over Meg's name. Aiden never understood why she couldn't just call her Meg like everyone else.

"Megum*i*," Aiden corrected, emphasizing the hard *e* sound at the end. "Or you could just call her Meg," he quietly added.

She glanced at him and then said around her fake smile, "I didn't know you were here."

"Well, Aiden needed help, so..."

The tension between them was something that Aiden wasn't expecting but suddenly recalled. He had forgotten that they always seemed so stiff around each other. He hadn't completely understood, or paid attention, to it before, but their discomfort was obvious. Now that he had outgrown the habit of ignoring what he didn't want to see, he was curious about the strain.

"Let me take those," Meg offered.

Becca pulled the boxes a little closer. "I've got it."

"Okay. Um, I'll go get Phil," Meg offered and disappeared up the stairs.

"*Mom?*" Aiden pressed.

"Do you have plates?" she asked, moving around him.

"There's a pack of disposable ones on the counter. I haven't bought any real dishes yet."

Her mood lifted. "Oh. We should do that soon. What else do you need?"

"Pretty much everything. We'll have to spread it out so I can afford to eat."

"I don't mind helping, sweetie."

Leaning on the counter, he watched her looking around his bare kitchen. "Mom, Meg and I are friends."

She turned to him. "That's nice, honey. It's good that you two could get beyond the past."

"But if I have my way," he continued, "we'll get back to being more. I miss her."

Becca inhaled sharply as she turned her attention to the food she'd brought. She didn't encourage him, but she didn't discourage him either. Her silence, however, spoke ten thousand words, and none of them good.

"What's your problem with her?" he asked.

"Nothing." She faked a smile as she faced him again.

"Yeah, I'm going to have to call bullshit on that. I saw your reaction to her when she came into the room."

"I was surprised, that's all."

He stared at her. "You used to have the same reaction back when we were dating. Whenever she was around, you always got a little bit frigid."

She tried to laugh off his observation. "That's not true."

"I hope it's not because of her ethnicity."

Becca gasped, as if shocked at the accusation. "I am *not* a racist, Aiden," she whispered harshly. "How could you say that?"

"Well, there's something about her that puts you off. If it isn't because she's Japanese, what is it?"

She didn't answer, and he didn't push because feet started pounding down the stairs, indicating their private conversation had to end. Phil and Meg laughed as she chased him down the stairs. Becca forced that frozen smile to her lips, and Aiden stood to watch the pair race across the empty living room. Phil reached the counter first and threw his hands in the air.

"Winner, winner, biggest piece for dinner," he announced.

Meg play-punched him in the gut. "Cheater."

"Whatever. Hey, Becca, thank for bringing pizza over," Phil said.

"Well, I had my reasons. I wanted to see how much progress you'd made." She slipped into her natural state of playing hostess and opened the pizza boxes. As the three painters lined up, she asked each what kind of pizza they wanted and served them. Aiden noticed that she tried extra hard to be courteous to Meg. Since he didn't have a table, they all leaned against the one unpainted wall and ate.

Becca asked about Harris and Mallory and Aiden's work, but she clearly struggled trying to find anything to say to Meg. Aiden hoped Meg hadn't noticed, but when he caught her eye, she lifted a brow and smirked just enough to let him know she had.

Clearly there as something there. His mother denied it was because of Meg's heritage, but the rock that was forming low in his stomach was telling him his suspicions were true.

sh

It was well after midnight when Meg decided to throw in the proverbial towel and washed the paintbrush she'd been using. Her hands were cramped, her back hurt, and she'd inhaled so many paint fumes over the course of the day, she didn't think she'd ever smell anything but the chemicals again.

She set the paintbrush on the counter with the wet bristles hanging over the sink so they could drip dry. After drying her hands on a towel, she rolled her shoulders to stretch the muscles and looked around the kitchen. She never would have picked such plain colors, but the off-white really did work well in the room. The walls looked crisp and clean.

"What do you think?" Aiden asked, bringing his roller in.

"I like it. The color makes it look so bright."

He pulled the used roller off the handle and wrapped it in a plastic bag so it would still be wet and usable when they returned to finish the job sometime the next day. He was clearly brooding over something, but she couldn't put her finger on it.

"Whatcha thinking, Aiden?"

He set the roller aside and leaned against the counter. "I'm sorry."

She tilted her head. "About?"

"About my mom. I don't know what her problem is, but I'll tell her to get over it."

She sighed. He wasn't that stupid. He knew; he just didn't want to admit it.

"You know exactly what the problem is, Aiden. *I'm* the problem. Everything about *me* is the problem."

He opened his mouth, but she gave her head a sharp shake to stop him.

"The last thing your parents want is little Japanese grandchildren running around their yard for the neighbors to see," she said.

He looked like he was going to argue but thought better of it. "I'm going to talk to her. I really hope that's not her issue, because that's a pretty outdated point of view to have." Reaching out, he grabbed her hand and pulled her to him until she was inches away. He tucked a long strand of her dark hair behind her ear and stared into her eyes. "As for me, I'd be pretty damned happy to have little Japanese children running around my yard for the neighbors to see."

She didn't know what to say to that. Of all the plans they'd had for the future, they'd avoided any mention of children, but the image that danced through her mind was perfect. For a moment she thought it was the fumes she'd inhaled, but deep inside she knew better than that. Without thinking, she closed the distance between them and put her mouth to his. Four long years had passed since the last time she'd kissed this man, but her body remembered him.

The moment he wrapped his arms around her and pulled her against his chest, she responded the same way she had so long ago. She slid her arms up his chest and wrapped them around his neck, digging her fingers into his short hair. The strands used to be longer, easier to fist in her hand, but she didn't mind the shorter cut he kept now. She could still thread her fingers in and pull him closer, and that's exactly what she did.

He hugged her even tighter as he brushed his tongue over her lips. She parted them and let him in. The intimate exchange heated as he lowered one hand, cupping her ass and pulling her hips against him. Temptation was strong. If this continued, she had no doubt her bare ass would be on the counter as she let Aiden have his way with her. The image was so clear and appealing she almost begged him to make it real, but she wasn't thinking clearly.

She was tired and her emotions had been in a blender since he'd returned. He'd told her that he loved her. She'd admitted that she loved him. But they had to be smart about this. They had to be the grownups now that they hadn't been four years ago. And grownups thought things through. Screwing him on a whim on his kitchen counter was not thinking things through.

"Aiden," she breathed after breaking the kiss.

"Don't say it," he begged with a whisper.

"I have to go."

"You said it," he pouted. He put his forehead to hers and cupped her face. The gesture was so sweet and tender, she nearly melted. "Thank you for helping me today."

"You're welcome."

He didn't release his hold on her, and she didn't pull back. "Text me when you get home," he said. "I won't sleep until I know you're home safe."

She smiled. "I will."

He dipped his head and kissed her lightly. "I love you, Megumi Tanaka."

He very rarely used her full name. She probably would have taken offence, but she knew he'd done so then to let her know he loved everything—even her heritage—even if his parents might not.

She put a bit of distance between them then. The sincerity in his eyes was obvious. She didn't doubt his love for her in that moment, and another bit of her defenses fell. "I love you," she whispered. "Good night."

She was to the door before he called out to her. Turning, she lifted her brows in question.

"How do you feel about furniture shopping now?"

Holding her breath, she considered his offer and then nodded. "I think I'll have time this week. Call me."

CHAPTER TWELVE

*M*eg shouldn't have kissed Aiden the night before. She shouldn't have let him hold her in his arms. She shouldn't have let herself melt into him or let his warmth seep into her soul. She shouldn't have allowed herself to imagine their children running through that house. She'd barely slept a wink thinking about him and their kiss and how good it felt to be with him. And how stupid it was to trust him again.

Sinking into her sofa, she pulled a blanket around her, but it didn't come close to the comfort of his embrace. He was right there, so obviously waiting for her to accept him, and she wanted that. More than anything, she wanted to go back in time and have what they had lost, but she just couldn't take the leap. She was standing on the edge, looking down, but the fear of landing flat on her face again was too great.

Are you guys up? she texted to Mallory and then sank back on the sofa as she waited for a response and let thoughts of Aiden fill her mind. The beep of an incoming response distracted her.

Mallory's reply was, *Aiden?*

Of course.

Bring breakfast. And coffee.

Meg was wearing old yoga pants and a sweatshirt, but she didn't care. She was planning to go paint at Aiden's later anyway. She wasn't concerned about ruining the old clothes. She stuffed her feet into her shoes and debated which fast food drive-through to hit before going to Mallory's. She arrived at her friend's house with a bag filled with hash browns, sausage biscuits, and a stack of pancakes for Jessica. She balanced that with a drink carrier filled with three cups of coffee and one orange juice.

Mallory opened the door still in her pajamas with Harris in the wrap around her chest. "Feed me," she said dramatically.

Meg set her offerings on the kitchen table. "Where's Phil?"

"With Aiden," Mallory said, as if it were the most obvious thing ever.

Meg widened her eyes. "What? Why?"

"Because he sent a pathetic text too."

"*Hey.* My text wasn't pathetic. I just asked if you were up."

"I read between the lines." She held up the pancakes with questions in her eyes.

"For Jess."

"She stayed at Kara's last night. These are mine." She tore open a pack of syrup and drowned the fluffy cakes. "I know about last night. About the kiss. Very romantic."

Meg frowned. "It was. Kind of."

Mallory stopped her fork before she could fill her mouth. "Why only kind of?"

Meg unwrapped a biscuit and lifted the top off. She had a habit of checking her food before eating it since she hated eggs with every ounce of her being and more than once she'd gotten a mouthful without realizing it. Satisfied that the food was as she ordered, she picked it up, ready to take a bite. "His mom."

Mallory creased her brow. "Becca was there?"

"No. Well, not physically. We were discussing how she doesn't like me. Aiden reassured me that he didn't care, and then...I kissed him."

"Awww, that's so sweet. But why wouldn't Becca like you?"

"We don't know for certain, but we're pretty sure she'd rather Aiden dated someone a little less...non-white."

Mallory took time to sip her coffee before responding. "I don't know them well, Meg, but I can see how they'd have a problem with that. Becca and Jim are a bit old-fashioned. Jim more so than Becca. But you and I both know Aiden doesn't feel that way. If he did, you guys wouldn't have dated back then and he sure as hell wouldn't be so determined to win you back now."

Meg creased her brow. "He's not—"

"He is. Trust me. He is. If his parents can't accept you, I really believe he'd choose you."

"Yeah," Meg dropped her breakfast. "He all but said that last night. That's part of the problem. I don't want him to have to do that. A big reason he came back here was to bring his family together. I don't want to make that more difficult for him. It's not just his parents, Mallory. We don't have the best history, you know."

"But you've both changed since then, Meg. The Aiden I know is nothing like the man you used to tell me about. And you're not the Meg who used to cry over him for hours at a time."

She wrinkled her brow. "It wasn't hours."

"*Hours.*"

She gave up denying the accusation. She guessed Mallory was right, and she would know better. By the time Meg got done crying, she'd be chin deep in tissues and usually tipsy on the wine Mallory always served to ease her pain.

"You're scared he's going to hurt you again."

The lump that suddenly lodged in Meg's throat nearly choked her. "I want to trust him. I do. But whenever I start thinking about the future we could have, I remember the past that we *did* have."

Mallory reached out and wiped a tear from Meg's cheek. "The thing about love is that there are no guarantees. It's one day at a time, and not every day is a good one. Some days it takes everything you have to believe in it. Aiden made a mistake, Meg. He paid for it. He suffered for it as much as you did. He misses you like crazy."

"He *left* me," she whispered. "He was supposed to love me, and he left me."

"I know." Mallory grabbed a few napkins and thrust them at Meg. "He hurt you. But right now, you are hurting yourself. You're just sitting in limbo. You aren't moving forward, and you aren't letting go. You're stuck in this in-between. You have to do something. Either believe in him or don't, but don't keep sitting here being torn about what could be and what was. You are both different than you were then. Do you love him?"

"Yes." She dragged a napkin under her nose.

"Do you want to be with him?"

She knew the answer but didn't want to admit it. "I don't know."

"Megumi," Mallory said with the same tone she used to warn Jessica that her patience was wearing thin. "Do you want to be with Aiden?"

She was again bombarded with images of sharing his home with him, of seeing their kids running around, of a dog that would need to be walked and groomed and fed. Of the perfect future that she had never been willing to admit she wanted. "Yes."

"So...do it." Mallory grasped Meg's hand. "Listen to me. Sometimes second chances lead to regret, but sometimes second chances are all that you need to find some happiness. If Aiden is choosing you over whatever issue his parents have, then let him choose you. Trust me, if Becca and Jim choose to continue alienating themselves from their family because they think they are somehow superior to everyone else, then that is their choice. Aiden wants to be with you, Meg. He really does."

Meg sniffed, wiped her face, and sighed. "When did you get so smart?"

"Oh, honey," Mallory cooed. "I've always been the smart one."

8h

Aiden left the café where he and Phil had shared breakfast and went straight to his parents' house. He and Meg were going to get back together, he was confident of that, and sorting this whole thing out with Phil had made him see things far more clearly. Aiden's mother wasn't the problem. His mother had probably never been the problem. It was his father.

That was a conversation Aiden wasn't sure he was ready to have, but the distance between him and his dad was only going to grow if he didn't do something about it. If Phil's suspicions were right, that Becca's response to Meg was more about Jim's feelings toward her, then Aiden needed to go straight to the source of the issue and end it.

He wasn't surprised to find his dad sitting in front of the television watching a game. That seemed to be how he spent most of his time these days. Things didn't used to be like that. His dad had never been overly affectionate, but he had been present. Sometime in the last five or so years, he'd started retreating, and nobody had seemed to notice or at least dared to mention it.

Sitting on the couch, he looked at the recliner that had been deemed his father's. Nobody else ever sat there. "Hey, Dad."

"Hey."

His mom appeared in the door and offered Aiden a weak smile. "I wasn't expecting you until later."

"I just had breakfast with Phil. Since I was out, I thought I'd drop by."

"Oh, well, I can be ready to go in just a few."

"Actually, I'd like you to have a seat too, Mom."

She stared at him for several seconds before sitting on the other end of the couch. Leaning forward, Aiden clasped his hands together and took a deep breath.

"Before I moved to New York, I didn't pay much attention to a lot of things. Mostly because I was immature and self-centered. I didn't give things much thought. Being in the city taught me a lot more than what I was expecting to learn. One of those things was how important family is. Several things played into my decision to come back to Stonehill. One of them was that I wanted to try to make things right with Megumi."

His dad scrunched up his face. "That Chinese girl?"

"Japanese, Dad. She was born in Japan."

"Aiden," his mother said softly, as if warning him.

"When Meg and I were dating," Aiden continued as if she hadn't spoken, "I noticed that you two treated her differently than you'd treated other women I'd dated, but I didn't really think about why. Until I noticed how Mom reacted to seeing her last night."

"Jesus," his dad muttered under his breath. "Boy."

"Meg and I are working things out," he said. "And I don't care how you feel about that. I love her. I've always loved her, and I made a huge mistake when I broke things off with her. If I have my way, Meg and I will be married and have a family someday. So I want to make one thing very clear. If you have a problem with her, then you have a problem with me, and you'd better address it with me right now."

He waited, but neither of his parents said anything. His mother had tears in her eyes, and his father's jaw was set. Aiden pressed his lips together and exhaled loudly.

"Do either of you have a problem with Meg?"

"Do you have any idea the kind of shit your kids will have to take if they're mixed?" his father finally asked.

"Dad," he said as calmly as he could, "we aren't living in the 1960s. Interracial couples are common now, and so are their children."

"What if she wants to give them Japanese names?" his mom asked.

He wanted to roll his eyes, but he'd opened this conversation so he could address their concerns. He wasn't going to mock them. "That's a decision between my wife and me."

"She isn't your wife," his dad muttered.

"*If* she becomes my wife and *if* we have children and *if* she wants to give them names that reflect their heritage, then that will be a decision between my wife and me. Whether I marry Meg or someone else, our children's names are our decision. No one else's."

"But...I can't even say her name," his mom said.

"Meg, Mom. Her name is Meg. You *choose* to make it more difficult than it is."

She looked shocked. "I was trying to show her respect by using her name."

"Well, to be frank, it comes across as if you're pointing out that she's different."

Widening her eyes, she gawked at him. "I told you last night that I'm not racist."

"I'm not implying you are."

"The hell you aren't," his dad muttered.

Aiden looked at his father. "What's your problem with Meg?"

"I don't have one."

He wasn't buying this. But he wasn't going to argue it. "Okay. Listen to me, I'm only saying this once. If you do have a problem, get over it, because if you make her feel uncomfortable, then she's not going to want to be around you, and if she doesn't want to be around you, I'm not going to force her. That means you won't be seeing a lot of me, either. Understood?"

"Understood," his mother whispered. His father didn't answer.

"Mom, if you want, I'd like your help buying some things for my house. Are you up for it?"

She blinked a few times before nodding. "I'll go grab my things."

Aiden stood and looked at his father, who had returned his attention to the television. "Dad."

Again, he was met with no answer. He left without another word, guessing he'd probably be seeing a lot more of his mother in the future than he would of his dad.

CHAPTER THIRTEEN

*M*eg hugged Harris more tightly to her chest when Mallory looked at him with puppy dog eyes. "He's fine."

"I know. There are bottles in the fridge."

Meg nodded. "I know."

"I'll keep my cell phone on all evening."

"I know."

Mallory continued staring at her baby. "Call if you need anything. Anything at all."

Lifting her brows, Meg turned her attention to Phil. She and Aiden had agreed to keep Harris while the rest of the Martinson-Canton clan went to Jenna's wedding. This was the perfect excuse for the new parents to get a break, but if Mallory didn't leave soon, they were going to be late.

Meg sighed and turned her body just a bit so Mallory couldn't take Harris from her. "Get her out of here so you guys can enjoy the wedding. Please."

Phil grabbed his wife's hand and pulled her toward the door. "We'll be back in a few hours, Mallory. Meg and Aiden can handle it."

"I know they can," she whined.

"Go. Have fun," Meg said. "I promise this little guy will be right here waiting for you to get home."

Mallory gave her son one more kiss before following Phil out the front door.

Once they were alone, Meg turned to Aiden and laughed. "I give her two hours. At most."

"I give her half that. She's probably going to run out of there the moment Jenna and Daniel say 'I do.'"

Meg giggled as she looked at the bundle in her arms, but she couldn't deny his assessment. Mallory hated being away from Harris. Meg didn't blame her. If she could sit and hold this sweet baby boy all day and night, she probably wouldn't want to stop either.

"Your mommy is crazy, little man. Yes, she is." Walking Harris to the portable crib set up next to the sofa, Meg eased the swaddled baby down and patted him for a moment before sitting on the couch where Aiden had plopped down and reached for a slice of the pizza that had arrived just minutes before they managed to shoo Phil and Mallory out of the house.

Meg had assumed they'd watch a movie with their dinner, but he sat back and started filling her in on when the furniture they'd selected would arrive. Juggling their opposite schedules hadn't been easy, but they'd managed to find a few times to meet up and look for the basics for Aiden's house. They'd selected a gray couch and love seat set and a contemporary coffee table. He had brought his flat screen TV from his old apartment to hang on the big empty wall that the couches would face. He said his mom wanted to help him buy dishes.

Meg didn't know, and didn't *want* to know, if he'd confronted

Becca on their joint suspicion that she didn't like Meg because of her race. If that was the case, Meg didn't know how she and Aiden could actually work around that. If they did get back together, and she couldn't deny that's where this seemed to be headed, a wedge was going to be driven between Aiden and his family. Meg didn't want that.

He'd been working so hard to bring his family together, she didn't want to be the reason his mission failed. The fear was on her shoulders, though, and she couldn't pretend it wasn't weighing her down.

"Have you seen your parents since Christmas?" he asked as he added another slice of pepperoni and jalapeño pizza to her plate.

His side only had pepperoni. Peppers—any kind, including jalapeño peppers—gave him indigestion, something she used to love to tease him about.

"No, but Mom calls every day. I think she's worried if she doesn't, I won't talk to her anymore. Which isn't the case. She just calls before I can. I haven't talked to Dad, though. I don't know what to say to him."

He swallowed a big bite before asking, "Are things with Aya still going well?"

She smiled. "Yeah. I hadn't realized how much I missed her. I hope we can stay on an even keel, but I'm always waiting for something to blow it all up. That's what usually happens."

"I'm glad things are getting better. I, um..."

"What?" she asked hesitantly.

"I talked to my parents." He glanced at her and shifted in his seat, letting her know he was uneasy sharing this with her. "I told them that someday I'm hoping you and I will be a couple again, and if they had a problem with that, they needed to get over it."

"And how did that go over?"

"Mom heard me. She said she doesn't mean to call you *Meg-Meg-Meguma*." He smiled when Meg laughed. "She thought she was showing you respect by using your full name. Even if she can't figure out how to say it."

"And your dad?"

Aiden dismissed the mention of his father with a shrug. "He's never heard me in the past. I don't expect this to be any different."

"*Aiden.*"

"It's fine."

She searched his face. His eyes were sad. Determined but sad. "No, it's not. You came home to—"

"Get my life back on track, and a huge part of that was making us better. You and me."

"At what cost?" she whispered.

Putting his hand on her knee, he held her gaze as he said, "At any cost. I didn't realize it before, but I think the real reason I came home was to fix this. This is what matters to me. *You* are what matters to me."

His words warmed her heart but didn't ease the guilt settling in her stomach. "You don't know how hard it is to be estranged from your family, Aiden. It's like a shadow that hangs over you all the time. You don't want that. I don't want to—"

"I gave them the choice to accept us or not," he stated, cutting her off. "I think Mom will try. Dad… Dad is who he is. Stubborn and narrowminded. He's going to do whatever he wants. But so am I." He put his hand to her cheek and gave her a soft smile. "And what I want is sitting right here next to me."

Meg returned his smile as he leaned in. He kissed her lightly, not with the passion they'd shared the night before, but she felt the exchange all the way to the pit of her stomach. This was happening. She and Aiden were happening. Again. And she couldn't stop it if she wanted to, but the thing was, she didn't. All she could hope for was that she didn't live to regret it.

He broke the kiss and sighed. "You taste like jalapeños."

"That's not the jalapeños, sweetie. I'm just too hot for you to handle."

Aiden grinned. "I'm not going to argue with that." Taking her plate, he set it on the coffee table and wrapped his arm around her so he could pull her closer. He dipped his head down and kissed her again. This time, he jumped right into a heated kiss.

Meg was tempted to crawl into his lap, straddle his thighs, and delve into a pretty serious heavy petting session, but Harris let out a little wail, reminding her they weren't alone. Laughing quietly, she put her finger to Aiden's lips. "Behave, or I'll send you home."

Aiden eased his hold on her and sat back. Meg grabbed her plate and took a big bite of her pizza. The heat of the peppers was nothing compared to what she was feeling for the man sitting next to her, though. She wanted him. More than she wanted to admit. More that she wanted to want him.

"How are things going with your mom and Kara?" she asked, hoping to distract them both. She ate as he told her about the trip the museum the women took and his mom's hopes of helping Kara distract her toddler. He sounded hopeful, and Meg was happy for him. By the time they both finished eating, most of the pizza was gone, and they'd again fallen into easy conversation.

They'd been sitting there just about an hour when keys jingled in the door. Aiden smirked, looking cocky, but Meg didn't call him on it. He'd been right. Mallory had lasted less than two hours. As soon as the door opened, she practically ran in. She barely acknowledged them before rushing to the crib and scooping up the still-sleeping baby.

"Well," Meg said to Phil, "looks like all is right in the world now."

He didn't take his eyes off the scene of his wife checking on their newborn. "Seems like it."

"How was the wedding?"

"Very nice," Phil said. "Marcus didn't even glare at his new brother-in-law once."

"Because Mom would have killed him on the spot," Mallory said, nuzzling Harris.

"Did you even make it to the reception?" Meg asked.

Phil shook his head. "Jessica stayed. Annie and Marcus will bring her home later."

Meg sighed. "Mally, he didn't even wake up. Go back and have some fun. We'll call if we need you."

"No. And you guys just leave me alone," Mallory said before pressing her lips to Harris's head. "I missed my baby."

Meg hadn't voiced her concerns, but she knew in that moment it would be a long time before Mallory was ready to return to work. She missed having her best friend and co-conspirator in the office, but she couldn't begrudge Mallory's unspoken decision to stay home with Harris. Meg would probably do the same thing if she had a family of her own. "Do you want this pizza?" she asked Phil as she stood.

"Leave it. We might have some," Phil said.

Aiden followed Meg to where they'd hung their coats by the front door. "It's early yet. Wanna go grab something to eat?" he asked as they bundled up.

"We just had pizza." She looked back but didn't call out to Phil and Mallory. They were already lost in their little world. Stepping out into the cold, she looked up at the night sky, wishing there would be a break in the cold winter.

"How 'bout a drink?" He shoved his hands in his pockets.

A few weeks ago, that nervous habit of his made her want to kick him in the shins. Tonight, she found it adorable. Too adorable. And a little irresistible. "You're a doctor now, Aiden. If you get caught drinking and driving, you're going to be in a world of trouble."

"I'll have a soda. It's not even nine o'clock yet. I'm not ready to go home and ignore my parents."

She looked at the house, debating. They were walking on thin ice here. They'd both admitted to still loving each other and had shared a few hot kisses. She didn't want to jump in too fast, but damned if she wasn't tempted to do just that.

"Want to go to Sam's?" she asked. They used to frequent that bar in college, but she hadn't been there in a long time. She doubted the dark, dingy scene had changed much though.

Aiden's eyes lit with excitement. "Yeah. Sounds good."

She nodded toward her car. "I'll meet you there."

"Last one there has to buy." He practically ran in his SUV to try to beat her.

Meg chuckled to herself. Damned if she wasn't tempting fate right now, but it felt oh so right.

sh

Sam's was just as Aiden remembered—loud, dark, and smelled like stale beer. Being there brought back a million memories. The bar had been one of his favorite places in college. Sitting with Meg now, he couldn't help but remember how most of those nights ended—with them naked and moving together in a sensual dance that still made his body react when he thought of it.

He was convinced that no one had ever looked better in a pair of faded jeans and a fitted T-shirt than Meg. He'd had a hard time keeping his attention off her body while babysitting, but now it was nearly impossible to not steal glances at her whenever possible.

"What?" Meg pulled him from his memory.

"Huh?"

She grinned slyly, as if she had read his thoughts. Sipping her iced tea, she stared him down over the rim of the red plastic cup. Aiden was certain they were the same cups the bar had used four years ago. When she lowered her cup, she licked her lips and grinned at him.

He couldn't resist temptation any longer. He needed to touch her. If they were a couple, he would slide into the seat next to her and warp his arm around her. He'd kiss her head and whisper in her ear. But they weren't a couple. He thought that might happen sooner rather than later, but for now, he had no right to invade her space so intimately.

Taking her hand in his, he squeezed it tight. That would have to do for now, and since she didn't pull away, he was perfectly content with the contact. Looking around the bar, Aiden couldn't quite remember what it was about this place that had been so alluring to him just a few years ago. The air was too thick, too heavy, and the music was so loud that everyone was screaming just to be heard. He'd much rather they were sitting in a quiet restaurant. Or even better, on the couch at her apartment since his place still didn't have furniture.

This scene certainly didn't have the appeal it used to. Of course, he wasn't the same person he used to be. Instead of yelling over the music to Meg about how he was going to just play one more game of pool with his buddies, he wanted to talk to her. He wanted to hear her soft voice and feel her warm skin.

He almost laughed at himself. Yeah, he certainly had changed. The last time they'd been in this bar, he'd been so intimidated by his feelings for her that he was secretly trying to find a way out of their relationship. Tonight, he'd give anything to be able to say they were in a relationship.

She said something, but Aiden couldn't hear her over the music and yelling around them. He leaned across the table and cupped his ear. "What?"

"Stop looking at me like that," she said slowly so he could read her lips.

He smirked. He didn't really know how he'd been looking at her, but he imagined it was with amazement or tenderness or...longing. "No."

Meg laughed at his blunt answer and shook her head. Taking another drink from her glass, she turned her attention toward the dart board, where a group of guys were taunting each other mercilessly. That used to be Aiden and his friends. He had no idea how damned annoying he used to be.

Leaning even closer, he called out Meg, "Didn't we used to like it here?"

"We did."

"Why?"

She nodded toward the pool tables where a group of younger twenty-somethings were hanging out. Oh. Right. He used to hang out there too. With his friends while Meg sat at the table with hers. They used to come here together, but then they'd part ways until it was time to go. Another pang of regret hit him. He sure had wasted a lot of time.

The small dance floor stopped hopping when an Ed Sheeran love song started filtering from the speakers. A few dancers booed and headed for the bar, but most paired up and started moving to the slower beat. Standing, Aiden pulled Meg with him, leaving their half-full glasses on the table. She didn't resist, but she did give him a sarcastic smirk as he aimed for the small opening in the sea of bodies.

They had been doing a proverbial slow dance around their feelings for weeks now. Pulling her against him was just one more way they would be adding fuel to a slow-burning fire. He guessed she knew that as well as he did by the way she would grin every time he sprinkled a little gasoline on the embers.

His body remembered the feeling of holding her the moment she slipped into his arms, as did his heart. Meg still fit so perfectly against him, like she'd been made to fit there. She draped her arms over his shoulders, and he pressed his lips to her forehead. Swaying slowly, he felt like his soul was mending a bit more with each move they made. Hugging her more closely to him, he cupped the back of her head and squeezed her tightly.

There were still so many things he needed to share with her. So much he needed to tell her about his time away. About why he couldn't cut it in the city. About the emotional wounds he was still trying to heal. The way the events that had unfolded before his eyes had stayed with him even now.

He was going to have to find the strength to tell her more than how sorry he was that he left her.

"I'm not sure this is a dance as much as a hug," she said in his ear.

Aiden chuckled. "Close enough." Turning his face into her hair, he inhaled her scent. Not the same as he remembered, but just as soothing to his battered soul. The loud bar and stale beer smells disappeared, and all that was left was Meg. He was lost in her, and he would have stayed that way if she hadn't pulled back.

She searched his eyes as if seeking some kind of truth. He wasn't sure if she found what she was looking for, but she leaned in and kissed him lightly. Taking his hand, she led him from the cramped dance back to their table, where she grabbed her coat from the back of her chair. Aiden helped her slide the down-stuffed material up her arms and then followed her outside.

"I think we've gotten old, Megumi," he said as he draped his arm over her shoulders.

"Speak for yourself, Doctor."

"Were you having fun?"

She grinned. "Not as much as I used to." Stopping in front of her car, she turned and rolled her head back to see his face. "If I invite you to my place to enjoy a drink without the crowd and the noise, are you going to take that the wrong way?"

He shook his head. "Nope."

"Are you going to expect more than just a drink?"

He shook his head again. "Nope."

"Okay. Then you may follow me home."

Aiden resisted the urge to give her a fist bump. Being alone with her was all he'd wanted in the first place. He ran to his SUV and reminded himself the entire drive to keep his desire for her in check. He didn't want to push or make her feel uncomfortable. He needed to be patient and let her set the pace, even though part of him just wanted to scoop her up and take her to his house. He wanted to set her down on his threshold and tell her that's where she belonged and that's where he needed her to be. And that's where she needed to stay. Right there with him.

Somehow he didn't think she'd appreciate that kind of archaic approach. Meg was too smart and independent for that kind of thing. He'd have to bide his time until she walked into his house and said that was where she belonged. He just hoped she didn't wait too long. They'd already wasted so much time. No, not they. *He.* He had wasted so much time.

At her apartment complex, he parked in the spot next to her car and jumped out of his SUV, eager to get back to her. She met him as he rounded the front of his vehicle and led him to the secure door of her apartment building. As they climbed to the second floor, he took her hand and entwined their fingers. His need to touch her grew by the minute.

The atmosphere inside her apartment grew tense as they discarded their jackets and hung them on the hooks by the door. Aiden sat on the couch and watched Meg move to the kitchen and grab two bottles from the fridge. When she sat down, she sat close enough that their knees touched. Such a basic touch shouldn't have thrilled him like it did.

He stared at the amber-colored bottle she handed him for several long seconds before setting it on the table. "If I drink, I can't drive, remember?"

The sly grin on her face returned. "I remember."

Was that her subtle way of asking him to stay? He eyed her, waiting for clarification, as his heart pounded in his chest. Excitement, anticipation, fear. He didn't know which emotion was driving the increase of adrenaline, and he didn't care. All he knew was that no other woman had ever made his pulse race like Meg.

"I have a couch," she whispered. "You've slept on it before and we both came out unscathed."

"That was...before."

"Before?"

"Before I kissed you. And you kissed me."

She nodded. "Yes, but I feel quite confident that we could manage sleeping in the same apartment without crossing lines we shouldn't cross. Unless...you find me so irresistible that you can't be trusted."

He considered her words for a moment before saying. "I should go."

She didn't argue, so he stood and took the few steps to the door.

"Don't go," she said.

He looked back, but she was picking at the label on her bottle.

Finally, she looked at him. "Not yet. Just stay for a little longer. I have soda if you prefer."

His heart did a funny jump in his chest. At the same time, his stomach dropped to his feet.

"I want you to sit here and talk to me."

"Okay." He resumed his seat. "What would you like to talk about?"

She giggled. "I don't know. I didn't make a meeting agenda. If you give me a minute, I'm sure I can scribble something down."

Aiden laughed as he leaned back. "I'd like to suggest that we discuss how I was trying to be responsible and leave."

"You can't be responsible if you stay?"

"It will be a hell of a lot more challenging," he admitted.

She grinned, and the urge to kiss her almost overtook him. Damn it. She was playing with him. She was toying with him and loving it.

Aiden exhaled loudly. "Gastroenterology."

Meg stared blankly. "What?"

"You wanted to talk. Let's talk. Topic: gastroenterology."

"You want to discuss digestive issues?"

"I want to discuss that I've been considering that I should have become a specialist instead of a general practitioner. I've always been fascinated with the digestive system. Now that I'm taking time to think about our future—"

"Our future?" she asked.

"I have been giving specialized medicine more thought," he finished without acknowledging her question.

"You want to go back to school?"

"I wouldn't have to. I just have to do a fellowship. I'm sure I could find one in the city."

"Have you checked?"

"No," he said, realizing that was something he probably should have done before sharing his rambling thoughts with her. "Well, not yet, I haven't. I'm not going to be doing this right *now*. Not anytime soon, actually, but once I get settled I think I should narrow down my specialty."

"Which you want to be..."

"Gastroenterology," he stated with a confident nod.

She blinked at him several times before that slow grin spread across her face. "Aiden?"

"Hmm?"

"Am I making you nervous?"

He looked at his hands before he realized she'd asked that because he was rambling like a fool. "Maybe a little."

"I don't bite," Meg said in a teasing tone.

Aiden smirked. "Really? You used to."

She grabbed a decorative pillow from beside her and hit him with it as she laughed. He grabbed it and pulled it against his stomach. He wasn't joking, which was what made the comment even funnier. Meg took a drink before setting the bottle on the table and sitting back. She pulled her feet up and sat with her legs crisscrossed as she faced him.

She rested her head in her hand and propped her elbow against the back of the couch to hold her up.

"What was she like?"

Aiden creased his brow. "Who?"

"Whoever you dated after me?"

He thought back. "This feels like a trap."

"It's not. I've been curious about the woman who took my place when you moved."

He sighed. "She was reckless. Inattentive. Carefree. Not even remotely interested in something long-term."

"She was perfect for you."

"She was there," he clarified, "when I wanted her. And gone when I didn't."

"She was perfect for you."

He chuckled. "Yeah, this definitely feels like a trap."

"I dated this guy whose nickname was Madman," she said with a wistful smile.

Aiden pressed his lips together so he didn't laugh. "Madman?"

She nodded. "He was a total badass. Tattoos all up and down his arms. Long hair, full beard."

"You're lying," he said.

"Nope. We met in a bar. He was impressed by how many tequila shots I could do. He said my petite body shouldn't have been able to handle that kind of liquor. I pointed out that I'm Japanese. I have *saké* in my veins."

He did laugh then. "Bullshit. You don't even like *saké*."

"Then I dated this guy that used to cry all the time. At the movies, at weddings, anywhere, anytime. He was sweet and all, but I couldn't handle that. I dated a few other guys here and there, but as Mallory likes to point out, I sabotaged them all."

"I can't imagine why you'd ever want to end things with Madman," he said with sarcastic curiosity.

She playfully glared at him before her face softened. "Because none of them were you. That's why. I think in I knew deep down, or at least I hoped, that you'd come home some day and we'd end up here. Trying to figure out what the hell happened and if we wanted to get it back."

"I want it back," he said, not giving her a moment to doubt that.

She lowered her gaze, and a sense of dread knotted in his gut. Whatever she was about to say to him was not good. He hoped she wasn't about to shoot him down, but if she did, he had to admit he deserved it. He deserved her rejection.

"I need to tell you what happened after you left."

His fear of rejection turned into something else. The racing of his heart was no longer because of her close proximity but because the nervous energy rolling off her pierced his skin and set him on edge. "What?" he whispered.

"I don't want you to feel like it was your fault. I think everything was coming to a head before you left, I just didn't understand what was happening."

He grabbed her hand. "Meg?"

"I crashed, Aiden. I mean…the bottom fell out and I fell with it. I couldn't get out of bed. I couldn't go to class. I couldn't do anything. I quit going to work and paying rent. I got evicted and had to stay with a friend, but it wasn't long before she got fed up with me sitting on her couch doing nothing. She kicked me out, so I moved in with someone else. When I met Madman, he was reckless and wild and didn't care about anything. He was perfect for me at the time."

Aiden's stomach tightened so hard he could feel the acid rising. "Depression?"

She nodded. "I answered an ad for some college girl looking for a roommate. That's how I met Mallory. She saw what I was going through. She recognized it and started pushing me to talk to her." Meg grinned. "Man, I trashed you so much. My life had fallen apart, and I blamed you. My parents blamed you. Everyone blamed you because I was Megumi Tanaka, brilliant and focused and studious. Until I wasn't. And that happened right after you left, so it was easy to pin it on you."

"I should have seen it," he whispered.

Meg shook her head hard. "No. Aiden, I didn't even see it."

He clung to her hands. "But I should have. Hell, maybe I did." The admission hit him hard. He'd always assumed her quiet, introverted nature was just how she was. "You used to work so hard at school, and then sometimes you'd just stay home night after night, and I justified it as you needing to recharge."

"I did. I still do. I push myself to keep going. I'm on antidepressants, and some days I still struggle to get out of bed, but now that I know, it's a bit easier to fight the demons that try to keep me down."

"I'm sorry."

She shrugged. "It explains a lot, you know. Why I could never stand up to my parents. Why it was so much easier to just get walked over by everyone instead of standing up for myself."

"Everyone including me." That familiar feeling of guilt and shame returned. "I'm sorry, Meg."

"You don't need to be."

"Mallory saw it. She got you the help that you needed. It should have been me, but I was too blind, too self-centered."

Meg tightened her hold on his hands. "I think it was a frog in boiling water situation, Aiden. You didn't see it because you watched it slowly build. Mallory saw it because by the time she met me, I was completely unraveling. She couldn't ignore what was happening because when she walked into my life, it was already a disaster."

"Are you in therapy?"

"Not anymore. I've learned my triggers and I try to avoid them."

"And then I come back and shake everything up."

She laughed, but he saw the sudden sheen of tears in her eyes. "That was...unexpected."

He used his hold on her hands to pull her to him. She practically rolled across the couch and into his lap. Hugging her tight, he wished he could go back and make things right. Make everything right, including seeing what he'd been too immature to see. "I'm sorry," he whispered. "I'm going to do better this time. I swear."

Just like she'd done a thousand times in the past, Meg curled against him. The meaning was different now. Years ago, he thought she was a bit too clingy at times. Now he felt the need to protect her and heal the wounds he couldn't see. He bundled her up, kissed her head, and vowed to never let her feel alone again.

CHAPTER FOURTEEN

*a*iden looked at the little Valentine's Day gift box he was planning to give Meg. The silver bracelet wasn't fancy, but he thought it was enough to let her know that he was serious about starting over with her. He just had to decide *when* to give it to her. When he picked her up? Over dinner? When he took her home? He couldn't quite decide the proper etiquette for giving his not-quite-girlfriend a present.

He put potatoes in the oven to bake and set the table for two. He set the box on her plate. Then removed it. Then put it back. Standing back, he stared at it, started to remove it again, and then laughed at himself, debating if that was the best way to give her the gift he'd selected for her. He was still having that internal debate when she called out to him.

"In here," he answered.

She smiled at him as she appeared from the entryway. His desire for her intensified. She'd worn a short flowy dress and heels that, despite being sexy as hell, seemed like a serious hazard. One wrong move, and he'd be taking her in to have her ankle X-rayed. He wasn't going to complain, though. She looked amazing.

"I thought you made reservations," she said as he moved into the kitchen.

He dropped two steaks on the preheated pan. They sizzled and the scent of his marinade instantly wafted through the air. "I reserved this night for you. That's the same thing. Kind of."

She bit her lip. "Aiden?"

Suddenly, his grand gesture seemed wrong. She didn't seem as excited as he had hoped. "I wanted to be alone with you. All the restaurants are going to be bustling and loud. I didn't want that. Are you mad?" he asked, hearing the uncertainty in his voice.

Her smile grew as she shook her head. The tenderness in her eyes answered for her, but she said, "No. This is probably the sweetest thing you've ever done. It's wonderful."

Relief rolled through him. "Maybe not *the* sweetest thing. But probably in the top ten. I stopped at the store on the way home and grabbed steaks, potatoes, and a bagged salad. Sound good?"

Rounding the counter, she wrapped her arms around his neck. "It's perfect."

"I hope so."

She kissed him lightly. "What can I do to help?"

"Pour the wine."

She grabbed the bottle of cabernet sauvignon and filled the two glasses sitting next to it. He couldn't help but watch the way her lips caressed the glass and her tongue darted over her lips. Damn it. He was in so much trouble with this woman. The good kind of trouble. The kind of trouble he'd been scared of the last time they were together but was happy to embrace now.

"Very nice," she said after taking a sip.

He was about to agree before he realized she meant the wine. He smiled, more because he was so amused with his inability to think straight when Meg was so close to him. "You like that?"

She held her glass to him to let him have a sip, but he ignored her offering and slid his arm around her waist to pull her to him. He placed a light kiss on her lips and sighed with contentment.

"Delicious," he whispered.

Meg giggled, and the sound rolled through him.

"What else can I do?" she asked, looking around.

"Give me more of those."

Meg easily slid into his arms as he kissed her. Their kiss excited him in a way that convinced him there could be a lot more of that going on before the night ended. Her hair was swept into a loose bun, as if to deliberately tempt him to release the single clip holding it in place. The way she leaned into him made him think she had the exact same hopes for their evening.

Lust was in the air, and not just his. But before things got too heated between them, he had dinner to finish cooking. "Medium on the steak, right?"

"Yes, please. Want me to serve the salad?"

Aiden grinned at her, feeling a little shy. As soon as she walked to the table, she'd see the white box with the red ribbon sitting on her plate. "Um, yeah. If you don't mind."

She got out two bowls from the cabinet and filled them with bagged salad and then looked at the dressing options he had bought. "You know me too well. This herb and garlic infused oil is perfect."

He was pleased he'd gotten the right thing. "I admit that I had to think about that for a few minutes. I couldn't quite remember which was your favorite."

"This is perfect." She closed the fridge and tore the bag open.

His anticipation grew as she filled the bowls and carried them, along with the bottle of dressing, to the table. He knew the moment she saw the box; she slowed her stride and looked back at him.

"Aiden," she said with a sweet little coo. "I didn't think we were doing presents. I didn't get you anything." She put the bowls and dressing on the table. Picking up the box, she turned and pouted. "I feel bad."

"No…" He crossed the kitchen to her. "Do not feel bad. I wasn't expecting anything. I got this for you because I wanted to."

She gave him a soft smile, but then it spread. "Can I open it?" she whispered.

"Please do. I've been so anxious about this all day."

Meg put her fingertips to his cheek and kissed him softly. "Don't be anxious. Whatever it is, I'm sure it's wonderful."

"Only one way to know," he said.

She plucked the ribbon free and then eased the top off. He watched her face, taking in her reaction as she moved the thin paper aside and exposed a silver bracelet with a little heart-shaped charm.

"Oh," she gasped. "Aiden, this is so beautiful."

"Are you sure? If you don't—"

"I love it," she stated before he could imply otherwise. "I absolutely love it. Thank you." She looked at him, and her eyes said all he needed to know. She really did love it. And she loved him. He could see the affection shining. She set the box aside and held the bracelet out to him. "Help me?"

He unhooked the little clasp and wrapped the chain around her wrist before securing it. "Perfect," he said. Bringing her hand to his lips, he kissed her knuckles. "Just like you.

She wrapped her arms around his neck and hugged him tight.

"Thank you." She planted a soft kiss on his lips. "I'm so happy I'm here with you tonight."

He had to swallow the surge of emotions her words brought. "I am too, Meg. More than you can ever know."

She nodded toward the kitchen. "I think those steaks are nearing medium well."

"Oh, shit." He rushed around the counter to check on their dinner.

8h

Meg couldn't have asked for a better Valentine's Day date with Aiden. He'd made everything so damned perfect. She was a puddle of mush inside. As they finished putting their dishes in the sink, he suggested they watch a movie, but she had other plans for the evening.

This thing between them was growing every day. The more time she spent with him, the more time she *wanted* to spend with him. Denying that this was going anywhere but where she had been fantasizing was pointless. So was denying that she wanted him so much she could barely see straight whenever she was around him.

So when he turned to head toward the living room where the television had been mounted on the wall, Meg grabbed his wrist and stopped him. He looked at her curiously, and she felt her cheeks warm. She never used to be so bold, but this was just one of the many changes he was going to have to get used to. She had learned to go after what she wanted, and right now, she wanted him.

"I don't want to watch a movie," she said.

Aiden's lips twitched. "Oh. Well, what do you want to do?"

She could tell he was testing her, so she smiled and answered honestly. "I want to go upstairs and have sex. Preferably with you."

He chuckled, clearly shocked, but he recovered quickly. "Since I'm the only other person here, I guess I'll have to do."

"I guess so. Think you're up for it?"

Another laugh slipped from him. "I'm sure I can rise to the occasion."

This time she giggled and pulled him to her. Letting the amusement and teasing fade from her smile, she lightly touched his cheek and kissed him. "I want you," she whispered against his lips. "If you're ready."

"I'm ready." Wrapping his arms around her, he pulled her hips to his. His erection confirmed what he'd said. "I'm more than ready."

"So take me upstairs," she breathed. Her heart started to race as he brought her hand to his lips. A moment later, he turned and guided her toward the stairs. As Meg finally gave in to what she had been fighting for so long, she couldn't hold back. Every emotion she'd been hiding erupted within her, suddenly making her nervous about what she had been so adamant that she wanted.

They walked into his bedroom, and he spun her. "Are you sure?"

"Yes, I'm sure."

That was all she needed to say. He pressed his mouth to hers, and all the tenderness his previous kisses had contained dissolved. His mouth was demanding and hungry, as if he'd been starving for her. His tongue slid between her lips and his fingertips dug into her as he crushed her against him. He eased the clip from her hair, letting the long strands fall so he could brush his fingers through them.

All the anger about their breakup, the desperation of missing him for so many years, all the love, the longing, and need, came pouring out of her as she hungrily kissed him. Pulling him closer, she gave him all the unspoken permission she could. This was *going* to happen. This was happening.

He slid his hand down her side to her thigh and under the flowy material of her skirt. His hands were hot against her, scorching her. She wanted more. She turned her head, letting his lips move to her neck, where he gave her the same passionate treatment. Running her fingers through his hair, she focused on the heat and wanting radiating through her.

Aiden lifted her just enough to carry her across his room and lay her on his bed. Almost instantly, his body crushed her against the mattress. His weight and heat were almost too much, but at the same time she didn't think they could ever be enough. All she wanted to think about right then was the love Aiden was offering her.

Easing down her body, Aiden assaulted her breast through her thin shirt, roughly teasing her nipple with his hot mouth through the barrier while tugging her skirt up her leg. Sighing when she finally felt his warm skin against her, she moaned his name.

He massaged her thigh as he continued trailing his kisses lower. Meg swallowed hard and closed her eyes when his breath warmed her stomach. Moving her hands from his shoulders, she reached above her head and wrapped her fingers around the bars of the headboard. The moment his kiss fell on the inside of her thigh, she knew there was no going back. Not that she wanted to.

Aiden gripped her hips and lifted her body to him as he ran his nose along the center of her panties, inhaling deeply before pressing his mouth against her. Meg hissed and tightened her hold on the wrought iron that was keeping her grounded. He kissed her thigh again and then gently nipped her skin with his teeth, causing her to gasp and thrust her hips up.

Sliding his hand up her leg, he pressed his thumb in a slow circular motion, obviously determined to torture her. "Aiden," she panted. "You're being an asshole."

He laughed softly. "I know."

"So stop." She exhaled a trembling breath when he moved the material aside and dragged his tongue over her. "Oh, that's better. That's *so* much better."

He took his time, as if remembering her scent and taste, before he finally sat back. They were both breathless, and the air of teasing was gone. This was serious business now. She reached for the buttons of his shirt, quickly undid them, and then pushed the material off his shoulders. When he tossed his shirt to the floor, she moved to the button of his slacks. Aiden rolled over onto his back and pushed his pants down, removing his boxers and socks at the same time, and then tossed it all to the side.

As he did that, Meg lifted her shirt over her head and then fell back to shove her skirt down. When he rolled back to her, she was there, in the black satin bra and panty set she'd bought just for this moment.

"Jesus," he breathed. "You're so perfect, Meg." Rolling onto his side, he used her hip to roll her into him. "I don't know how I ever found the strength to walk away from you."

"Shh," she hushed, pressing her fingertips to his lips. "It's in the past now. It's all in the past."

"I missed you so much I couldn't breathe sometimes," he whispered. "I was such a fucking fool. I won't be again. I swear to you, I will never make the same mistakes again."

"I believe you, Aiden."

"I want to make love to you."

She grinned. "I'd like that very much."

Reaching behind her, he released the clasp keeping her bra in place and caught her exposed breast with his hand. Moving down, he covered her nipple with his mouth as he pushed her back on the pillows. A moan escaped from deep within her as he moved between her legs, crushing her with his weight. A moment later, he tugged her bra completely free, and she dug her hands in his hair as he suckled her breasts.

"Tell me you have condoms," she whispered.

He stretched over her to get into the drawer of his nightstand. While he put protection in place, she removed her panties and leaned back, parting her legs as he returned to her. When she lifted her hips, her body all but begged for him, practically pleaded for him to finish what he had started.

Pulling her arms from his shoulders, he pinned them above her head and looked down at her. His expression seemed to mirror her own emotional turmoil needing to be released, needing to go somewhere before it exploded. She leaned up and kissed him, gently biting his lip, tugging his mouth toward hers. Slipping his tongue into her mouth, he dueled with her momentarily before leaning back enough to see her face.

Meg held his intense stare as he thrust into her. Holy crap... He still fit so perfectly inside her body. She wanted to cry from the happiness of having him there again. Wrapping her legs around his, she welcomed each thrust. Over and over again, she rolled her hips to meet him, only stopping when she felt like her mind was separating from her body.

She closed her eyes and grunted as an orgasm rolled through her. Her lungs seemed to stop working until she finally managed to gasp for air. Aiden groaned as he rolled onto his back, taking her with him. Straddling him, Meg rolled her head back as she ground against him. When he roughly squeezed her breasts, she looked down at him, finding an even more intense look on his face. He didn't have to say what he was thinking. Evan after all this time, she could read his mind and his body. He was nearing the edge and wanted her to jump off with him.

She put her hands on his chest for support while she moved faster and harder, helped by the hands that had held her hips. He thrust up and threw his arms around her, pulling her to him, and she knew he was about to finish. The thought that she could still bring him pleasure carried her with him and a second climax rocked through her.

True to the teasing he'd given her, she sank her teeth into his shoulder as she cried out. Not hard enough to hurt the poor man, just enough to keep her from losing her damn mind from the pleasure that was literally taking her breath away.

When she was finally able to relax, Meg swallowed hard as the emotions that had been brought to the surface were at the boiling point. She had to close her eyes and take a long slow breath to keep her tears at bay, but she couldn't stop the shaky breath that escaped her. She couldn't remember another time in her life when she had felt so much all at once. She wasn't sure where it was coming from or what to do with it. All she knew was that it was consuming her. Trying to control herself, she held him tighter and buried her face in his shoulder.

Wrapping his arms securely around her, Aiden kissed the top of her head, holding her until his breath returned to normal. Running his hand through her hair, he kissed her head again. "I love you. More than anything in this world. Do you know that?"

"I do."

He hugged her even closer. "I'm sorry. I didn't mean to be so rough with you."

"You weren't." Meg shook her head as she lost the battle and her entire body shuddered with a sob. "It's Mallory's fault."

He stroked her hair. "Maybe we shouldn't talk about Mallory right now."

"I never used to cry. She did this to me." She sat back. "I'm sorry. I'm just... I don't know how to explain it."

He pulled her even closer. "Overwhelmed?"

"I guess."

"Me too," he whispered and kissed her head. "Are you sorry this happened?"

"No." Leaning back, she looked down at him. "Are you?"

"Are you kidding? This is the happiest I've been in a long time." When she laughed, he smiled and brushed her hair from her face. "That's not what I meant. What I meant was having you here in my arms, loving me, makes me happy."

"I knew what you meant."

"I love you, Megumi."

Smiling as another sob escaped her, she kissed him. "I love you. So much. But if you leave me again, I'll never forgive you."

"I know." He pulled her back to him. He didn't say the words, but she knew that was his way of promising her he wasn't letting her go again.

CHAPTER FIFTEEN

*M*eg jolted when she felt movement next to her. She needed a moment to orient herself, but once she did, she remembered falling asleep in Aiden's bed. Rolling onto her side to face him, she watched him run his fingers through his hair. He huffed out a long deep breath that sounded far more stressed than she would have expected, given they'd made love earlier.

Her heart twisted in her chest. She didn't want to keep doubting him. She believed that he wanted to be with her, that he loved her, but she couldn't forget that she had believed that once before. When he pushed himself up and disappeared into the bathroom, the doubt in the back of her mind started to crush down on her.

She knew this feeling. This was something she had experienced far too often in her life. She used to let it consume her. This was the feeling that had dragged her down so low that her life imploded. Fighting this self-doubt was a constant struggle, even now, but she had learned that she had to fight it if she didn't want to drown in it.

Pushing herself out of the warmth and comfort of his bed, she followed him. Taking a deep breath, she knocked on the door. "Aiden? Are you okay?"

"Yeah. I'll be out in a minute."

He didn't sound okay. His voice was tight, strained. Stressed. She just hoped it wasn't because he regretted the steps they'd taken. Looking at the bracelet on her arm, focusing on the little heart charm, she tried to tell herself that he wouldn't have bought her the gift if he weren't serious about moving forward with her.

But damn those voices in the back of her mind.

She returned to the bed and turned on the dim side table light. Fluffing her pillow, she set it against the headboard and leaned against it, fiddling with the charm on her wrist as she waited for him to return. When he did, the anxiety on his face was obvious. Her heart sank to the pit of her stomach.

"What is it?" she asked, terrified to hear his answer.

He offered her a weak smile, and she could have sworn it was the exact same look he gave her all those years ago. "I just don't sleep well these days," he said.

She didn't believe him. The look on his face was more than restlessness. "Aiden?"

He slipped under the sheet and scooted closer until he could rest his cheek on her thigh. Suddenly the fear that he was going to leave her faded and she realized there was something else going through his mind. He pressed himself so closely to her, she thought he must be trying to crawl inside her body. That was another feeling she was too familiar with.

She used to wish she could hide inside him. She'd sit in his lap and he'd hold her, and all her problems would fade. He hadn't even known that's what he was doing for her, and she felt the need to do that for him now. Wrapping her arm around him as much as she could, she tried to soothe him with her touch.

"Talk to me," she whispered. "What's wrong?"

Aiden sighed and burrowed his head deeper into her lap. "I'm haunted, Meg. Truly haunted."

"By what?"

He tightened his hold on her. "You were right. About the shit I'd see in New York. That I wasn't emotionally prepared to deal with those kinds of things. Rapes, gangs, child abuse and neglect, human trafficking. And I don't mean once in a while. I mean every day. Every goddamned day, Meg. And I couldn't do anything to save them. I could tend to their injuries, but I couldn't save them."

"I'm sorry," she said.

He was quiet for a moment before continuing. "There was this little girl. Her name was Anita. She was beautiful and so sweet. She had these big brown eyes and long brown hair. She reminded me of you in some ways. I think that's why I felt so responsible for her. After the second time she was brought to the ER, I started to suspect abuse. After the third time, I went to my supervisor so we could file a report. I told her she was going to be safe. I promised her that she would okay. I guess I thought the system would protect her."

Meg bit her lip. She didn't have to think too hard to know where his story was headed. She stroked his back and tried to comfort him.

"The next time she was rushed in, her bastard of a father had beaten her so bad her skull was fractured."

"Oh, Aiden," she whispered.

"I visited her every day until she died. I told her how sorry I was, but...that didn't matter, Meg. Nothing I did mattered. She died. I should have prevented that."

"No," she insisted. "Aiden." She pulled him until he shifted enough to look up at her. Her heart broke at the reflection of tears in his eyes. "You tried. You filed a report. You did what you could."

"It wasn't enough." He rolled onto his back and stared up at the ceiling. "Coming home wasn't just about fixing things in my family or even reconciling with you. Nothing I did there was enough. Nothing I did there would ever be enough. I couldn't process that kind of failure day after day, Meg. I'd lose my mind if I had to spend the rest of my life patting broken people on the head and sending them on their way, knowing nothing I'd done had made a damn bit of difference."

"You made a difference," she insisted.

He draped his arm over his face as if to hide from her. "No. I didn't. I wanted to, but I didn't. Whenever I close my eyes, I see them. I see the hundreds of broken and battered people I failed. When I sleep, I hear little Anita crying because she'd been hurt by her parents. Again. I see her," he whispered.

Meg had to swallow her tears when his voice broke.

"I see her in my sleep. She's going to haunt me forever. And I deserve to be haunted."

"Stop," she insisted. Sliding down in the bed, she pulled him onto his side so she could see his face. Stroking his cheek, forcing him to look at her, she said, "You did what you could. You aren't a social worker, Aiden. You aren't the police. You're a doctor, and your job is to report abuse. Which you did. The system failed her. Society failed her. Not you."

He didn't believe her. She could see in his eyes that he didn't believe her, but he seemed to appreciate her effort. Sliding to her, he hugged her close and kissed her head.

"I'm so happy you're here," he said softly. "You can't begin to imagine how much I regretted letting you go. I needed you so much more than I ever wanted to believe."

"I needed you too," she confessed. "You make me feel whole."

She was surprised when he choked out a little sob and pulled her closer.

"I'm not going to fuck this up again," he promised.

"I'm not either." She hugged him closer, letting him absorb the comfort he needed.

sh

The next morning, Aiden held up two DVDs as Meg filled their mugs with coffee. "Massive destruction by volcano or tornadoes?" he asked.

Meg pursed her lips together and twisted them to the side as she considered the options he'd offered. "Volcano."

"Sweet!"

He was so thankful for the normalcy of the morning. He had known that he'd have to talk to her about his ongoing issues with the things he'd seen in the city, but he hadn't planned on telling her last night. Once he'd started rambling, he couldn't stop. The emotional dam seemed to break. She'd held him for a long time before they were finally able to go back to sleep.

He feared she'd want to talk about his continued struggles, but she was kind enough to let it rest. At least for now. He guessed she felt the same kind of relief that he hadn't pressed the issue of her depression. They both had struggles and issues they would have to work with as they went, but he was confident they were in a good enough place to face whatever challenges life presented to them.

He was going to make certain they were.

By the time he got the movie started, she was settling on the sofa with their mugs. His heart nearly overflowed at the site of her in his T-shirt and boxer shorts. This was one of the things he'd missed he most. They'd had their first cups at the table while eating pancakes and chatting about how they should spend their day. They agreed the more time they spent on the couch drinking coffee and watching disaster movies the better.

Aiden sat next to where she'd curled up and rested his hand on her knee. They'd developed a love of movies like these long ago. The cheesier the so-called special effects and overacted dialogue, the more they loved them. Borderline B movies had somehow become their thing. If she wasn't watching cooking shows or shows about people renovating houses, they were likely indulging in some cheap flick about a natural disaster or monster wreaking havoc.

"This is terrible," Meg said, but she smiled as she did.

Aiden turned the bracelet on her wrist until he could rub the little heart between his finger and thumb. "Should we take bets on who lives to the end?"

"That's too easy." She took a sip and then pointed to the overly handsome actor flirting with a woman. "He'll make it to the end. She's going to die. She's definitely going to die."

He dropped his hand to her knee and drank his coffee as the dramatics on the screen played out. Terrible computer-generated graphics and a worse script kept them entertained through the pot of coffee.

They were about halfway through the first movie when Meg stretched out and put her head on his lap. That was it. Bad movie forgotten. He stroked his fingers through her hair, traced her ear with his fingertip until she giggled and swatted his hand away, and brushed his hand up and down her arm.

"You know when I say that I love you," he whispered, "I mean I'm passionately, insanely, head over heels in love with you."

Her eyes filled with obvious affection as she turned her face up to his. "And when I say I love you, I mean that even though you're an idiot, I can't imagine my life without you."

"Hey..." He poked her stomach, and she flinched, laughing in that way that always tugged at his heartstrings. So he poked her again. And again, until she wriggled out of his lap and jumped up.

"Don't do it," she warned.

They both knew he wouldn't listen. This was one of their favorite games. He charged her, hugging her against him as she squealed. Hefting her up, he put her over his shoulder and carried her back to the couch. He flipped her onto the cushions and stretched out on top of her. She parted her legs, making room for him, all the while playfully protesting the impending attack.

Aiden gently pinned her hands above her head and lifted his brows. "Take it back," he warned.

"No."

Leaning down, he pressed his lips to her neck and blew a big raspberry against her skin.

"Oh my God! No!" Laughter took away any seriousness to her words. "Aiden! Stop!"

"Take it back."

"Never!"

"Take it back," he said lightly, "or I'm going to smother you in kisses."

Her laughed quieted. "Liar."

"I'll do it."

"Go ahead and try."

He put his mouth on hers and pushed his tongue into her open mouth. She lifted his shirt while he tugged at hers until they separated long enough to discard their clothing, and then his lips were on her neck. She moaned his name, fisted his hair, and encouraged him to move lower. He didn't need coaxing; he was more than happy to flick his tongue over one of her nipples.

What he really wanted was to be in her, to be deep inside her, moving with her as she clung to him and called his name as she'd done a dozen times the night before. He hadn't had nearly enough of her. He'd never get enough of her, but he couldn't take her just yet. His condoms were upstairs.

Lifting her against him, chest to chest, he gripped her thighs as she wrapped her legs around him.

"You can't carry me all the way upstairs like this," she said.

"Watch me," Aiden countered.

He'd rounded the edge of the sofa and the corner that would have taken him to the stairs...if his mother hadn't been standing there with her mouth hanging open and a bag from a fast food joint dangling in her hand.

"Mom!"

She took a gasping breath. "You...you didn't answer when I knocked. I thought you were still in bed. I thought..." She lifted the bag, her eyes still wide. "I brought breakfast."

"Yeah. Um. Mom, why don't you just..."

"I'll leave it here," she said. She glanced around before setting the bag on the floor and started for the door. "Uh, nice seeing you again Meg-*ooh*...Meg."

"Nice seeing you, Becca," she said, her voice light with laughter.

The door closed behind his mother, and Aiden eased Meg's feet to the floor. She crossed her arms over her breasts as if his mother was still there. Her eyes were wide and her cheeks bright pink. "What the hell just happened?"

Aiden tried not to laugh, but he couldn't stop a chuckle from slipping through his lips. "Um. My mom walked in unannounced and very nearly caught me having sex with my girlfriend."

"Oh, man," Meg moaned. "I'm going to die." She dropped her face. "I'm so glad she didn't show up five minutes from now."

Leaning forward, he tilted her face up and kissed her. "I need to shower. I feel icky." Turning her toward the stairs, he guided her up to his bathroom. He didn't have to ask if she wanted to continue where they'd left. It was pretty damn obvious his mother had clearly killed the mood for both of them.

CHAPTER SIXTEEN

*M*eg could barely stop laughing long enough to tell Mallory about Aiden's mother walking in on them as they were headed upstairs. "I didn't see her face, but I can totally imagine."

Mallory put her hand to her chest as laugher roared from her. "Oh my God. That is hilarious!"

"No," Meg said around her giggles, "it's not. It's really not. She already hates me. Now she has all the more reason."

"Oh, please. Aiden is a grown man with his own house. She's the one who walked in unannounced. That'll teach her." Still laughing, she stirred her coffee. "Remember when I walked in on Mom and Marcus's heavy petting session when I moved back home? Lord. That taught me to always knock before entering. Now Becca knows. Life lessons aren't always easy."

Meg's laughter eased as she shook her head. "Poor Aiden. I can only imagine the conversation they're having his afternoon."

Mallory smiled warmly. "I'm just glad that you guys finally got back together. I'm so happy for you."

Meg huffed out a breath as she looked at the bracelet on her arm. "I missed that big old fool."

"I know you did. Are you still worried about him leaving you?"

She shook her head. "No. Well, not much. I mean, he just bought a house. He can't very well walk away from that, can he? He could break up with me anytime, but at least he won't be disappearing without notice anytime soon."

"Relationships don't come with guarantees," Mallory said. "You just have to trust in them."

"Not the easiest thing for me."

"I know. But you're going to try, right?"

She nodded. "Yeah. I'm going to try. And I'm going to try to make things right with my parents. It's not going to be easy, but I have to. I see Aiden trying so hard with his that I have to do the same."

Mallory patted her hand. "As long as you don't let them tear you down again. You've come a long way. I don't want to see them take away from all the strides you've made."

Meg smiled. If anyone knew how much Meg really had grown in the last few years, it was Mallory. She'd been through all the ups and downs with her.

Mallory grabbed her phone when it chimed.

"What?"

A wide smile spread across her face. "Jenna's in labor. She's already dilated to seven."

"Go."

Putting her hand to the bundle secured against her chest with a wrap, she shook her head. "No. I'll go visit after she has the baby."

"Put your child down and go," Meg stated firmly.

"I can't."

Meg rolled her eyes. "How are you ever going to come back to work if you can't even leave him long enough to go visit your aunt in the hospital?" Her heart kicked in her chest. She had suspected as much, but the words hadn't been spoken. She pouted dramatically. "*Mallory*. You're not coming back, are you?"

Mallory shrugged. "I'm not ready. Phil and I have decided that I'm going to extend my maternity leave. *Indefinitely*. I've already talked to Mom and Marcus. I told them to give you my office so you can get out of that dinky space we stuck you in when you started. They're going to talk to you about it Monday."

Meg stuck out her bottom lip even farther. "It's not going to be the same without you."

She kissed Harris's head. "I'll go back sometime. Just not right now."

"Okay. I get that. I do. But right now, your aunt is having *her* baby, and you should be there. Give him to me."

Mallory sank back in her chair before huffing out a breath. "Just wait," she said. "Someday, when you and Aiden have kids, you're going to feel the exact same way."

Meg smiled. Not only because she suspected Mallory was right, but the idea of having Aiden's kids filled her heart even more than it had been already. Pushing herself up, she went to work on extracting Harris from his mother's clutches.

sh

Aiden opened the door to Phil and Mallory's house and spotted Meg with baby Harris on her shoulder. She turned and pressed her finger to her lips to warn Aiden to be quiet, and he swore he saw his future. He felt as if his chest had erupted like the volcano in the horrible movie he and Meg had never finished watching.

She was a natural with Harris. And with Jessica. She was going to make an amazing mother. She bounced the baby and lightly patted his little back, keeping him calm as his weary eyes fought to stay open. His cheeks had filled out, and thin dark hair covered his head, allowing Aiden to imagine what their child might look like.

Damn. He was up to his eyeballs in fantasizing about Meg. Funny thing was, his fantasies had very little to do with sex. He guessed that's how he knew he'd finally grown up.

He set the bag of carryout he'd brought on the table. He had one thing on his mind as he moved across the room to her. Resting his hands on her hips, he kissed her lightly. The only reason he didn't hug her was because he didn't want to crush the baby.

"Have you heard from Mallory yet?" he asked.

She rolled her eyes. "Nonstop," she whispered. "She's seriously going through baby withdraw. Jenna's still in labor."

"How's she doing?"

"Okay as far as I know."

"And Jess?"

"She's in her room doing homework."

He took a step back. "I'll go grab her so we can eat."

Gripping his wrist before he could leave, she narrowed her eyes at him. "What's this wistful look about? You've had it since you walked in."

He closed the gap between them and rested his forehead to hers. "I could get used to this, Meg. To coming home to you." He smiled and covered the hand she had resting on Harris's back. "To this."

She tiled her head back, eyes widened a bit. "Slow your roll, buddy. We've been back together for like two minutes."

"That's long enough," he whispered. He gave her one more light kiss before heading down the hall to get Jessica. He had to knock on her door three times before she finally heard him. Her music was way too loud. He knew Phil and Mal didn't let her get away with that, but Meg was the "fun aunt," so he guessed Jess knew she wouldn't mind.

He wondered if that was a flash to their future too. Would he be the rule enforcer while Meg was the fun one? He thought that was probably going to be the case, but he didn't mind. Maybe he would when they actually had kids, but the idea of working through those parental problems was something he thought he would actually look forward to. As long as he was working through them with Meg.

"Hey," he said when Jess finally opened the door. "I brought burgers. Hungry?"

She blinked, and a big fat tear rolled down her cheek.

"Whoa," Aiden said, concern interrupting his dreams of the future. "What's going on?"

"I'm stupid." Her voice cracked and her lips quivered. "I'm so stupid."

Aiden didn't think twice about pulling her to him. He hugged her tight. "That's not true. What's going on?"

"I can't do my math."

If she weren't so upset, he would have laughed at the dramatics. Although if he had learned one thing about Phil's daughter, the girl was a natural at overreacting. "Well, you know what? I am awesome at math. Want some help?"

She sniffed and nodded. When she leaned back, his shirt was covered in tears. She looked at the wet spots and shrugged apologetically.

"Come eat," he said. "Then we'll take a look."

He followed her to the dining room, where Meg was pulling their dinner from the bag. Her face instantly sagged, but he held up his hands to stop her before she could get worried.

"She's having a bit of trouble with her homework, but we're going to worry about it after dinner. Right, Jess?"

She nodded but didn't have an ounce of her usual spunk. Dropping heavily into a chair, she accepted a sandwich with a muttered thanks and pouted as she unwrapped it.

"Meg's pretty good at math too," Aiden offered. "She used to help me when we were in school."

"You should have asked for help instead of getting so upset," Meg gently told Jess.

Her shoulders sank into an exaggerated slump. "You were too busy with the baby."

Aiden cast a glance at Meg, who flicked her eyes in his direction as well. He guessed she was thinking the same thing he was. There was more to Jessica's tears and downtrodden expression than her homework.

"I can help you and look after Harris," Meg said. "Just like your mom and dad do."

She huffed a little. "All Mallory does is hover around the baby."

Mallory? Aiden hadn't heard Jessica call her by name since the adoption was finalized in December. Poor kid must really be feeling the new baby blues. Biting into his sandwich, Aiden let Meg take the lead on reassuring Jess of her role in the family. As she did, kindly reminding Jessica of all the things her parents and grandparents still included her in, his notion that she was going to be a great mom was cemented.

She was patient and understanding but also pushed back when Jess wallowed a bit too much. But the time they finished eating, Jess was happier. Not as chipper as she usually was, but she seemed to be less out of joint about the fact that Harris needed a bit more attention than she did right now.

"We should talk to Phil and Mal," Meg whispered when Jessica went to get her homework.

"Yeah, but this is normal," he said. "I think all older siblings go through this at some point. We should remember that when we have kids."

He chuckled at the surprise on her face. Before she could retort, Jessica came back with the tablet she used for her online homework. Scooting close to her, he made it a point to keep his attention on her and her homework. He'd have to stare longingly at his girlfriend another time.

CHAPTER SEVENTEEN

*M*eg was going to kill Aiden. There had definitely not been a long enough span of time between his mother walking in on them very nearly having sex and this little lunch he'd organized. Smiling across the table, Meg searched the furthest corners of her mind to try to find something, anything, to talk to Becca Howard about, but all she could do was shrink more and more as the woman stared at her with the same deer in the headlights look Meg imagined was on her face.

"Meg," Aiden encouraged, "how was your morning?"

"Um, good. Good. I'll be, um, showing some houses this afternoon. So, you know, I was getting all that lined up. For a client."

Another stretch of awkward silence fell over the table. Aiden looked at his mom. "And how was your morning?"

"Um. Okay. I, um..." She leaned back and smiled when the waitress set her lunch in front of her. After they all agreed that everything looked wonderful, Becca focused on cutting her chicken.

Aiden bumped his knee against Meg's, and she glanced at him. Oh, yes. He was going to pay for this. If he'd waited a month, or even a week, the weirdness of this situation could have died down, but no. He just had to get it over with. Like ripping off a bandage, he'd said. It wasn't like ripping off a bandage. It was like drowning in pudding.

"Um, how's Stevie doing?" Meg asked, grasping the last neutral straw she could think of.

Becca cleared her throat, sounding just as uneasy as Meg felt. "Oh, you know. Football and video games. That's all he cares about right now. Typical teenage boy." She took a bite and chewed vigorously.

"Okay, this is painful," Aiden muttered.

No, no, no, Meg silently begged. She closed her eyes and sighed, knowing he was going to put everything out there on the table for them to dissect.

"Mom," he stated.

Meg grabbed his hand. "Aiden."

"Meg and I are back together. I told you we were going to get back together. We're a couple now. And couples have sex."

"Oh God," Meg moaned. She winced as she looked across the table at his mother. "I'm so sorry, Becca."

"Yes, Aiden," his mother stated. "I know what couples do. I have two children as a result of those particular activities."

"So let's all just laugh off the fact that you almost walked in on those...*activities*...and get over it."

Meg looked at Becca. "I'm sorry you walked in on that. I'm very embarrassed."

"Well," Becca said, "it's not like I didn't know you two...would... you know." She pushed her plate away and looked at Aiden. "Listen, I'm not trying to be insensitive. I think it's wonderful that you..."

"Got laid?" he asked lightly.

"*Aiden,*" Meg chastised. "Not helping."

Becca glanced from Aiden to Meg and back again. "Your father is never going to accept this relationship. You know how he feels about…" She exhaled, and her discomfort clearly ballooned. Sinking back in her chair, she shook her head. "He'll never accept this."

The air left the room like a vacuum. Meg couldn't breathe. She tried, but her lungs refused to work. She had suspected her ethnicity was an issue, but to hear his mother all but say it was like a kick in the stomach. She couldn't think of a damn thing she'd ever done to his father. She'd always been respectful. Always been kind to his parents.

There was only one reason she could think of. Her skin tone. Her facial features. Even though she could tell herself that was his father's problem, not hers, finally having confirmation of her suspicions cut at her. She hadn't felt like this since elementary school, when the kids used to pull the corners of their eyes back and ask her to make them eggrolls. Only, most of those kids had grown up and realized their mistakes. Some had apologized. A few had even become her friends as they got older.

But Aiden's father wasn't a child who didn't understand the impact of his attitude. He was an adult with a deep-rooted prejudice that he chose to act on.

Meg had had to build a tough exterior to get through being one of the only Japanese kids in elementary school. However, that exterior had softened as she'd gotten older. Her friends, her coworkers and, as far as she knew, her clients didn't think of her as different. They didn't see her heritage. They saw her. *Aiden* saw her. She hated that his parents didn't.

Aiden squeezed Meg's hand. "That's Dad's problem. Not mine."

Becca sighed dramatically, as if Aiden were being a stubborn child. "Are you really prepared to lose your father over this thing?"

"*This thing?*" Meg snapped without thinking. "I'm not a *thing*, Becca."

The woman actually had the nerve to look shocked. "I didn't mean *you*. I meant this relationship."

Aiden put his arm around Meg's shoulders and pulled her closer to him. "Yes," he stated simply. "I choose Meg. I will always choose Meg."

Meg had to blink back her tears. Partly for the sting she felt from his mother, but also because Aiden should never have to choose between her and his family. That wasn't fair. She patted his knee. "I have to get back to work," she said.

"Don't leave," he whispered.

She offered him a smile and, ignoring Becca, kissed him lightly. "I love you," she said under her breath so only he would hear. "But this is between you and your mother."

He made a show, she guessed to make a point, of cupping her face and kissing her again. "I love you," he said more loudly than she had.

"Meg, I—" Becca started.

She wriggled free from his hold and gave his mother an obviously fake smile. "It was lovely to see you," Meg said and slid from the booth. She tried to hold herself together, but by the time she walked into O'Connell Realty, tears had started to fall and her breath was coming in little hiccups. Since Mallory wasn't there for her to run to, she did the next best thing and went straight to Marcus's office.

He looked up, and that familiar paternal protectiveness filled his face. He might be Mallory's stepdad, but Meg had all but adopted him as her own. He stood and opened his arms. She collapsed against him and accepted the second most comforting hug she'd ever known. Aiden's hugs would always be number one.

sh

"I didn't mean to upset her," Becca said for the tenth time since Meg left.

Aiden pushed his plate away and rested his arms on the table. "I heard you, Mom. I just don't believe you."

She frowned at her half-eaten lunch. "She needs to know how this is going to impact you."

"No. You need to know how it's going to impact *you*." He leaned forward, his lunch also forgotten. "I wasn't kidding when I told you guys that I won't come around you. If you can't accept my girlfriend, you can't accept me."

She sighed. "It's not like you're married to the girl."

"*Yet*."

She did that scowl thing again and looked around the restaurant. "I know your father, Aiden. He'll never accept her."

"Will you?"

"Of course I will."

"You say that like I have no reason to doubt you." Sitting back, he nodded when the waitress asked if she could take his plate. Once they were alone, he tapped his fingers on the table to draw his mother's attention. She was looking everywhere but at him. Once she met his eye, he said, "You're going to apologize to her. And you're going to mean it. And you're going to find a way to fix this. Because if you don't, Mom, then you're going to have to live knowing that I'm happily in love with a woman I fully intend to marry and start a family with someday and that you aren't part of it."

She gasped and put her hand to her chest. She hadn't made that face since he'd told her that he was moving away. "*Aiden*."

"She means everything to me. More than I ever thought she could." Sliding from the booth, he dropped enough cash on the table to cover the three uneaten lunches. "Until you figure out how to earn her forgiveness, I don't think you and I have anything to say to each other."

He climbed into his SUV and debated if he should text Meg. Instead, he just drove to her office. As soon as he walked in, Dianna glowered at him. He hadn't expected anything less from Meg's coworkers. In fact, he would have been shocked if he hadn't been greeted with frustration.

He lifted his hands before she could launch into the attack so clearly written on her face. "I know. I shouldn't have invited them both to lunch. I didn't expect it to go quite so badly."

She softened that scowl on her face. "She's in the bathroom blowing her nose and fixing her makeup."

As if that were her cue, Meg opened the bathroom door. As soon as she saw him standing in the lobby, she stopped in her tracks and her lip quivered. Aiden's heart broke, but not because he was on the verge of losing his parents. To hell with them. He hated how much Meg was hurting.

Opening his arms, he gave her as much of a smile as he could muster. "I choose you," he said. "I'm always going to choose you."

She choked out a sad sound as she rushed him. He enclosed her in his embrace and kissed her head once, twice, a dozen times as she crumbled against him. Finally, he led her to her office and squeezed them inside the small space. Sitting her down, he kneeled in front of her and handed her a few tissues he pulled free from the box on her desk.

"I'm so sorry," he whispered.

Shaking her head, she put her hand to his face. "It's not your fault."

The guilt in his gut didn't ease. "I pushed this on you. I wanted us to get beyond the awkwardness of the other morning. I didn't think she'd go where she went. I'm absolutely humiliated by her behavior."

Meg wiped her nose as another round of tears filled her eyes. "Do you really think your parents are the only ones who have ever discriminated against me, Aiden? I've faced it all my life."

"But I'm the one who put you in that situation this time. I'm sorry. I'll never do it again."

"So you're just going to avoid your family for as long as we're together?"

"Not all of them. I have a little brother who is pretty cool when he can be pried away from his gaming system." He tucked her hair behind her ear. "Phil and Mallory are my family, right? They love you, Meg. Jessica thinks you hung the moon. Kara and Harry are my family, and they adore you. So, no. I'm not going to avoid my family. Not the ones who matter." His heart ached when his words seemed to be making things worse.

She sniffled and dragged the wad of tissues across her face again. "I don't want to come between you and your parents. You have no idea how much it hurts to have a rift in those relationships, Aiden. I'll never be close to my parents, and that hurts so much."

He cupped the back of her head and pulled her down until he could rest his forehead to hers. "My parents are wrong, and I won't stand by and pretend like what they are saying is okay. It's not okay. Even if you and I weren't together, even if I didn't want to spend my life with you, Meg, I wouldn't support their belief that we shouldn't be together. I would never choose my life partner based on the color of her skin or her ethnicity. I love you because you're the only person out there willing to put up with all my shit."

She laughed a little, and the pain in his chest eased.

"Well, somebody has to," she whispered.

"I want that somebody to be you," he said lightly. "And if anybody out there has a problem with that, that's not *our* problem.

Do you understand that? I don't care what they think. This is about us."

She leaned back and shook her head slightly. "This isn't some little thing we can overcome just because we want to."

"No, it's not. But it's not something that we can't overcome. It won't be easy, but we can do it." He looked at the heart pendant on her wrist, brushed his thumb over it, and silently vowed that he'd do whatever he had to do to protect her from this kind of pain again. Even if that meant cutting his parents out of their life. He would do that.

"I hope so," she whispered. "You should go. You have to get back to work, and I have clients coming soon."

"I'm not going anywhere until I know you're okay."

"I'm okay."

She certainly was trying to put on a brave front for him, but her eyes revealed how broken she felt inside. The depth of it worried him.

Leaning up, he kissed her, hoping to take just a little of her pain away. "When you leave here tonight, I want you to go home, pack a bag, and go straight to my house. Don't argue with me," he warned. "I need to hold you tonight. I need to make sure you know how much I love you."

"I do."

"Good. But I want to make sure. Would you please stay with me tonight?"

She seemed hesitant but eventually nodded.

"Thank you." Pressing his lips to her forehead, he mentally kicked himself in the ass one more time. As he stood, he pulled her to her feet so he could embrace her. "I'll see you tonight."

He left her there, hoping she could pull herself together enough to get through the rest of her day. Aiden drove away from her office, but instead of heading toward the hospital, he turned toward the town square and parked in front of the jewelry store where he'd purchased the bracelet he had so loved seeing her open on Valentine's Day.

The last time he'd been here, he'd bounced between that bracelet and a platinum band that had been woven into an infinity symbol. At the time, the ring had seemed like a bit too much since they had just gotten together, but after what he had put her through today, he needed her to know that he was committed to their relationship. To her. To the future they had promised each other.

The same saleswoman helped him, but this time, he opted to not have the gift put inside a little white box with a red ribbon. He had different plans for this particular gift. With the ring tucked inside his glove box, Aiden pushed through his afternoon, but the disaster that had been lunch stayed with him. By the time he got home, his stomach was burning from the stress. He could only imagine how Meg must have felt.

At some point, he was going to have to face his parents and let them know that new boundaries had been drawn. Until Meg was ready to see them, they weren't going to be allowed to just drop by his house. He wanted Meg to spend as much time in his home as he could convince her to, and he wasn't going to have her uneasy being there. His home, what he hoped would someday be their home, was going to be a safe place for her. She wasn't going to sit on the edge, worried that his mother might pop in unannounced.

He had failed to protect her from the pain of the world around her once. He'd be damned if he failed her again.

CHAPTER EIGHTEEN

*a*s much as Aiden insisted Meg shouldn't let Becca hurt her, she was heartbroken. But she was mostly hurting for Aiden. She had tried to talk it out with Dianna and Marcus, she'd even called Mallory, but their "screw her" advice wasn't easing Meg's stress.

She sat at her desk, staring at her cell phone, not quite believing what her heart was telling her. Finally, she clicked on the picture of her sister and waited for her to answer.

"Megumi," Aya said, as if surprised she would call.

Meg had to smile. She and her sister spoke every day now, usually talked around their problems and ignored the real conversations they needed to have, but they spoke. "Hey," she said. She hadn't expected another round of tears to find her, but they did. She blinked them back. "Are you busy?"

"No. I can take a break. What's up? You sound upset."

Meg swallowed hard. "I had lunch with Aiden and his mom today."

"What happened?" Aya's tone was instantly defensive.

Meg tapped a pen on her desk, trying to find the courage to

actually speak the words. "I always suspected they didn't like that I'm Japanese, but she confirmed it today."

Aya was quiet. Too quiet.

"He's not breaking up with me. In fact," Meg said, "he told his mom he doesn't want her around us until she can learn to accept me."

"He said that?"

"Yeah."

She was silent again, and Meg felt the need to continue to defend Aiden. This wasn't his fault. He didn't feel the same. He was hurting too. But she didn't have to say any of those things.

"Good for him," Aya said. "You know better than anyone it isn't easy to stand up to your parents, but he did. And he did that for you."

Meg had to do that stupid rapid blinking thing again. "I don't want to be the cause of him losing his parents."

"You aren't, Meg," she said with a tenderness that Meg hadn't heard from her sister for a long time. "You can't control what other people think or whether or not they accept you. There are always going to be people out there who don't see you as equal. For whatever reason. You have to find the people who love you and accept you. And Aiden does. Doesn't he?"

She sniffed, and her heart felt a little less broken. "Yeah, he does."

"That's what you have to focus on. It would be great if his parents came around, but if they don't and he understands that this is on them, then you have to do what you can to make the life you want with Aiden. You can't change their opinions. We both know that. We have both dealt with discrimination. There's no reasoning with people like that. Take the love that Aiden is giving you and run with it, Meg. His parents have no say in that."

Meg smiled. "How did you get so wise about matters of the heart?"

Silence came across the phone again. She was about to call out, see if she'd lost the connection, but Aya sighed loudly.

"I'm not as inexperienced in that area as you might think."

Meg actually reared back from the shock. She'd never known her sister to date, not seriously anyway. Aya was all about her career. "What? Wait. Tell me what that means."

"I gotta go, Meg. But listen, if Aiden loves you and is willing to stand by you, accept that. It's not as common as it should be."

Meg pulled the phone from her ear and confirmed that Aya had ended the call. "I'll be damned," she muttered, surprised not only by Aya's sound advice but by the confession that there was more to her than a lab coat and DNA splicing.

sh

Aiden had just changed into sweats and a T-shirt when the front door opened and Meg called out to him. The knot in his gut eased. Part of him had been terrified she wouldn't show. When she walked into the living room, she lifted two foam carryout containers. "I hope you didn't cook."

"I didn't."

"I swung by the café and picked up two meatloaf dinners. Jenna's not back full-time yet, but I feel pretty confident she's still doing most of the cooking. She makes the best meatloaf." She set them on the table and instantly moved to hug him tight. "I'm so sorry about today."

Aiden leaned back enough to look down at her. "Why are you apologizing?"

Rolling her head back, she said, "Because I was so caught up in how much your mom hurt my feelings, I didn't really think about yours. She hurt you too. And I'm sorry."

The rest of his stress faded away. Part of him had been worried she might use his mom's behavior as a reason to put distance between them. "Thank you, but I'm more concerned about you."

"I'm okay. I talked to Aya this afternoon. If anyone knows how tough it was growing up looking like an outsider in this town, it's her. She had to deal with the same crap I did. I feel better after talking to her."

"I'm glad." They sat at the table and thankfully changed the subject. As they ate meatloaf and mashed potatoes with the most delicious brown gravy Aiden thought he'd ever had, he was happy to soak up the normalcy of the moment. No talk of the past, of his parents, or anything else that had caused them pain. She talked about a beautiful house she'd toured with clients and how perfect it was for them. She was certain they were going to buy it, but the price was a bit higher than they wanted to go. Meg was confident she could negotiate a better price if they'd just take the risk.

He loved seeing the excitement on her face as she talked about how she could get the house price down. She'd never had that kind of fire when she talked about medicine. She'd never seemed so driven as she did now. He was so happy she'd found her way. He hated that she'd hit rock bottom first, but he had in his own way as well.

If he hadn't gone to New York, he probably never would have had the courage to really find himself and his way back to Meg. He probably would have lived the rest of his life skating by, not just in his career but in his personal life too. He couldn't imagine that his love for her would have run as deep now if he hadn't lost her and had to find his way back.

Meg stopped speaking midsentence and grinned at him. "You're not listening."

He chuckled. "I am."

"What'd I say?"

"That you've never been happier and you're so glad that we found each other again."

A brilliant smile crossed her face. "That's not even close to what I said."

"Well, that's what the sparkle in your eyes said."

She laughed and tossed her napkin at him. "When did you become such a sap?"

Sliding his hand into his pocket, he gripped the ring and, without letting himself second-guess, pulled it out and showed it to her.

Her smile froze as she stared at it.

Aiden didn't let the shock on her face deter him. "I was torn between this promise ring and the bracelet. I'd decided it was too soon for a promise ring, but after today, this is right. This is the right time, even if we have only been back together for a short time. I want you to know that you are my future, and when we're ready—a month or a year or two years from now—I'll replace this with an engagement ring."

She smiled but not the same brilliant happiness that she'd shown when she opened her bracelet. She focused on the thin band as she bit her lip.

"If you don't like it—" he started.

"I like it. I love it. It's perfect."

He swallowed as that rock started forming in his stomach again. "So why do you look so pensive?"

"Because you're right. We have only been back together for a short time, Aiden. And with your parents, and mine, not approving of this, things could get rough. Maybe this...maybe this is too soon."

"No," he stated without hesitating.

"Our parents are not going to be supportive. Mine blame you for me dropping out of school. They aren't going to approve of us being together any more than your parents do. That's going to weigh on us, Aiden. That's going to be a problem we have to face over and over again until they change or we..."

"We can overcome that, Meg. I really believe we can. As long as we overcome it together. I'm not going to let my parents hurt you again. I promise. If that means we don't see them, then we don't see them. I can accept that as long as I have you beside me. And I'll do my best to win over your parents, to prove to them that I'm worthy."

She laughed softly. "Well...I promise to only translate the nice things my parents say to you."

Aiden laughed as he slipped the promise ring onto her finger, cursing when the band stopped at her knuckle. It was just a bit too small. Meg took her hand from him and gave the ring one final push until it rested in place. She held it up for him to see.

"Now you're stuck with me," she said. "This thing is never coming off."

He put his lips against hers. "That's exactly how I planned it."

CHAPTER NINETEEN

The dread in Meg's stomach was like a boulder weighing her down. She took Aiden's hand before he could turn off the ignition. "It's not too late. We can run."

He glanced up at her parents' house and seemed to consider it. "We have to do this."

"We don't *have* to."

This had actually been his suggestion. He'd convinced her to have one dinner with her parents to try to smooth things over with them. If Aiden couldn't win them over, if they still blamed him for "ruining" Meg's life, then at least they had tried.

"Aya will be here," Meg said. "She is going to try to act as a referee if needed."

"Well, I hope it won't be needed, but I appreciate the offer."

"Hey," she said before they could get out of his vehicle. "I appreciate you doing this. I want you to know that. It's not going to be easy."

"We just have to stay through dinner."

She nodded, and they exited the safety of his SUV and held hands as they walked toward the house. She felt a bit like she was getting ready to face a gauntlet, but if she were walking into open combat, she couldn't think of a better ally than the man at her side.

Her sister opened the door for them. The way her face was drawn was not a good sign. She'd arrived first in an attempt to help diffuse any anger her parents had at this forced attempt at a friendly dinner.

Meg tightened her hold on Aiden's hand. "This was such a bad idea."

"We'll be okay," he said.

"They are not happy," Aya said quietly. "Dad says he's not hungry and to eat without him."

A cloud of disappointment washed over Meg. She wasn't surprised, just saddened by her father's rejection. Taking a breath, she braced herself. "I'll go talk to him." Pulling Aiden deeper into the house, she headed for the kitchen. Her mother might not have been happy, but she wouldn't be rude to Aiden. Maybe a little frosty and judgmental, but she would be kind. At least that's what Meg was counting on.

"Mom," she said, trying her best to sound casual. "You remember Aiden Howard."

Her mother turned and very nearly shot daggers from her eyes before smiling just enough to be considered a greeting. "I remember."

Aiden held his hand out to her. "Nice to see you again, Mrs. Tanaka."

She stared for a moment but finally accepted his hand. However, instead of asking how he was doing or offering him a drink, she turned to Meg. "Your father won't be joining us. He's not feeling well."

"I'll go check on him."

"Leave him alone, Megumi," her mother warned.

Meg didn't listen. She gave Aiden a supportive pat on his upper arm and left him to fend for himself as she faced down the real challenge. Her father. She found him in his office, stone faced as he stared at his computer screen. "Mom says you aren't feeling well."

He barely glanced at her.

Closing the door behind her, she sat in the chair across from him and waited. They could sit in cold silence all night if that's what it took. She twisted the ring on her finger, the one Aiden gave her to reassure them both that they could get over whatever hurdles they faced. She drew on that to find the courage to speak. "I dropped out of school because I never wanted to be a doctor, Dad. Aiden breaking up with me just gave me an excuse to start my life over. When I did, I chose to quit something I never wanted in the first place."

"To be a retailer."

"A real estate agent," she clarified.

"If you're going to be a real estate agent," he said with blatant contempt, "you could at least sell high-dollar properties, Megumi. You'll never be successful on the path you've taken."

"You know nothing about the path I've taken because you don't want to know," she said. She'd never been so honest with him before, and it shocked both of them. Meg tended to bow out of any confrontation with her father. She respected him. She loved him. She hated that she had disappointed him, but Aiden was right. The life they wanted was the life they were choosing. Her job was part of that. "I've made mistakes. The biggest one was going into medical school. I should have spoken up a long time ago, but I just wanted you to be proud of me. I'm not like Aya, Dad. I don't want the life that she does. I'm happy with my life. I'm happy with my job and the people around me."

"Including that boy who broke your heart."

She nodded. "We were both kids back then. We were too young to know what we wanted with our lives. We've learned some things since then. Both of us. All the best parts of Aiden are still there, the parts that loved me and supported me. The parts that pushed me to be a better person. Those are still there. The scared little boy who ran out, the one you still see, is gone. He's proven that to me time and time again in the last few months. He's proven himself to Aya. If you give him a chance, he'll prove himself to you and Mom too. But you have to give him a chance, Dad."

He shook his head. "You'd be a doctor now if it weren't for him."

Meg swallowed hard. She had avoided this conversation for a long time, but it was time to come clean. "I have depression, Dad. I was already spiraling out of control when Aiden left. That was just the final straw. I never could have finished school back then. I couldn't handle the stress. Not because of Aiden or because I'm weak, but because I just couldn't handle it. Maybe I could now because I'm stronger and I got help, but I couldn't handle it back then."

He stared at her, not responding to what she'd told him.

She sighed. "I know you want to blame Aiden because that's easier. I blamed him for a long time too, but the truth is if he hadn't been there helping me, I would have had hit the bottom a lot sooner. I was never going to finish. I couldn't. If you want to hang on to blame, direct it at me. The only thing Aiden did was get scared of a relationship that was getting too serious. He wasn't ready for how deeply we had grown to care for each other, and he ran. But I've forgiven him, and so should you."

He still didn't respond.

Standing, she ran her sweaty palms over her jeans. "The man I love and want to build a future with has come to dinner to try to make things right with my parents. He's uncomfortable and nervous because he knows you don't want him here. But he came anyway because he loves me, and he knows my family is important to me. He's setting aside his pride and coming here to face you, and he's doing that for me. I hope you will do the same." She turned toward the door but stopped and met his gaze as she tapped into the one thing Aiden had said that had stuck with her over the last few days. "If you make me choose between you and the future I want, I'll choose Aiden. Every time, Dad. I will choose Aiden."

She returned to the kitchen in time to carry out a pitcher of ice water. She filled the glasses and sat next to Aiden, taking his hand under the table and smiling. He was worried about her. She could see the concern in his eyes, so she did her best to swallow her hurt feelings and focus on enjoying dinner. Her mother sat quietly while Aya talked about her day, but this time instead of sounding like she was gloating, she was talking excitedly about a new development her team had made.

Aiden asked questions and seemed genuinely interested, but Meg's mother barely said a word. Meg didn't comment on her mother's obvious discomfort, but she noticed and wished she could do something to make this easier for Aiden. Meg was halfway through the food on her plate when her father appeared and stood at the head of the table. The tension in the room multiplied, but finally, he held his hand out to Aiden.

"I apologize for being late," Eiji said to his guest. "I wasn't feeling well."

Standing, Aiden shook the man's hand. "I hope you're feeling better. It's nice to see you again, Mr. Tanaka."

The men sat, and Aiden patted Meg's knee under the table. The mood around the table wasn't exactly easy, but it was a start. It was a hell of a start, and Meg was happy to take it. When her father looked at her, she smiled her thanks and passed him a glass of water.

sh

The next morning, Aiden opened the front door and instantly felt irritated. Leaning against the door, he frowned. "Mom, I told you that you can't just drop by anymore. Meg might be here, and it's best if you're not around her."

His words obviously stung her. Tears instantly filled her eyes, and she held up a box from one of the local donut shops.

"I'm here to say I'm sorry. To you and to Meg."

"She's not here."

"I wasn't..." She blew out her breath. "Are you really going to make me stand on your doorstep?"

He hesitated before stepping aside and gesturing for her to enter. She walked right to the kitchen and stopped as she looked at the two coffee mugs on the counter.

"I thought she wasn't here."

"She was earlier. But she's not now." He moved around her and grabbed the mugs, putting them in the dishwasher before facing her. "She works most Saturday mornings. Not all her clients can find time during the week to look at houses."

His mom opened the box and showed him the contents. "Chocolate-covered Long Johns," she said. "Your favorites."

He didn't want one, but he didn't have the heart to reject her offering, simple as it was. "Thank you."

She peered inside at the rest of what she'd brought. "I didn't know what Meg likes, so I got a variety."

"She's pretty well rounded in her donut consumption."

Becca smiled, but it was uneasy. "I wasn't trying to make Meg feel bad the other day. I don't share in your father's views, Aiden, but I can't change them either. You have to understand that he isn't going to accept Meg."

"He doesn't have to, Mom."

"But if he doesn't, you're not going to see him. Isn't that what you said?"

He sat at the table, dropping his cream-filled treat on a napkin. "That's right."

She sat across from him, in the seat Meg usually occupied, and twisted her hands together. "I understand, but I don't want that to extend to me. Please, Aiden. Stevie and I... Well, you know how your father is. We tolerate him, the same way we did when you were younger, but we know he's... He's closeminded and angry at the world for reasons nobody will ever really understand. I raised you and your brother to be kind and accepting of others. Obviously that stuck. I wouldn't have raised you that way if I didn't feel that way. You know that, don't you?"

"I don't know anything anymore, Mom. When Meg and I were first dating, you guys always had reasons why we never saw you, but I didn't really notice. I was too young and distracted by life to notice. But Meg did. She asked me once if you guys were racist."

Becca gasped at the word. "I'm not—"

"I laughed it off back then, Mom, but I can't now. Do you have any idea how much you hurt Meg?"

She pressed her lips together and had the sense to look ashamed of herself. "I wasn't saying that *I* couldn't accept her."

"It sure sounded that way."

"I just wanted you to know that...if you tell your dad you are choosing Meg over your family, he's going to take that to heart, Aiden. He's going to see that as a betrayal to him and all he's ever done for you. It will drive a wedge so deep between you, I don't know that he'd ever recover from it."

She wasn't being overly dramatic. She was right, and Aiden knew that. His father had always been one of those was old-school, family-above-everything types, but he was taking it to an entirely different level. He'd probably never forgive Aiden and never accept Meg. But Aiden had already made his choice, knowing his father would likely hold that against him for the rest of their days.

"I know, Mom."

"She's worth that?"

He didn't even have to think about it. "Yeah, she is. But this isn't just about Meg. What if we broke up and I started dating someone else Dad didn't approve of? Do I let his racism dictate everyone I care about?"

"He's not racist," his mother stated firmly.

"What do you call it?"

She opened her mouth, but no words came out.

"Exactly."

"He was raised in different times, Aiden. This town was different back then. We didn't have the diversity we do now. Change is hard for some people to accept. That's all."

"No, Mom, that's not all. It's hateful and it's hurtful to me and to Meg. I won't put her through that. I understand that you didn't mean to come across that way, but you did, and that's exactly how she took it. You have no idea the things she had to put up with growing up. The shitty things the other kids said to her because she looked different and had a different name. The hell of it is, Mom, someday I plan to have kids with her, and they're probably going to look different. Maybe they will have names that are hard to pronounce. Maybe they'll have to deal with some of the same things Meg had to and get called names like she did. I hope not, but if they do, I hope they'll be tough enough to deal with it. But sometimes bullying like that tears a kid to pieces and they need their family to love and support them through it. If you can't do that for your grandchildren, then you have no business being part of their lives."

Her chin quivered. "I can do that. I *would* do that."

"What about Meg? Are you willing to love and support her?"

Becca nodded.

Smiling, Aiden stood and opened his arms. She jumped up and hugged him.

"I love you, Mom."

"I love you," she said into his chest.

Leaning back, he put his hands on her arms and held her so he knew she heard him. "I need you to explain all of this to Meg. I can't make this right with her on your behalf."

"What if she doesn't forgive me?"

"She will," he told her. "Neither one of us wants a rift in our families. We both want you to be a part of our future."

"And your father?"

He shook his head. "Not until he can pull his head out of his ass and respect Meg for who she is. I don't see that happening. Do you?"

"No."

"You will always be welcome in our home, as long as you come with an open heart."

She hugged him again. "I'll apologize to Meg. I'll do whatever I have to do to make this right."

Aiden smiled as she pulled away from him. As much as he was willing to keep his parents at arm's length, his heart was happy she'd come around. He hoped his father did as well, but he wasn't expecting miracles. "I know you will. I think we should start with dinner tonight."

"Tonight?"

"If you can tear Stevie away from his game long enough, bring him too. About six?"

She rolled her shoulders back, as if mustering the strength. "What should I bring?"

CHAPTER TWENTY

*M*eg stood, arms crossed and brow arched, staring at Aiden from the master bath. Taking the toothbrush from her mouth, she spit and then returned to gawking at him. She was going for firm, but with her hair a tangled mess, standing in nothing but a navy blue panty and bra set, she didn't think she was pulling it off. Especially since he kept lowering his gaze to her breasts and smirking.

"Aiden," she stated. "You're being ridiculous."

"When's the last time you spent the night at your apartment?"

She didn't know. She couldn't recall. Weeks, maybe? "That's not the point." She returned to the sink and rinsed the mint-flavored paste from her mouth. Grabbing her pants, she slid her legs in and pulled them up but didn't button them. Snagging her shirt off the counter, she slipped her arms in and tugged it over her head as she returned to the doorway to finish nip this conversation in the bud. "We've been back together for like five minutes."

"Three months officially," he corrected. "But we were practically back together at Christmas."

She chose to ignore his spin on things. "Three months is not long enough for us to move in together," she stated.

"Yes, it is. This is what we want. What we both want."

"We have to be smart about these things this time, Aiden." She didn't mean to throw the past in his face, but she had, and seeing him wince made her regret it immediately. "I just mean, we should take things slower. Be sure."

He crawled from the bed and crossed the room to him in nothing but a fitted pair of boxers. "I've never been more sure of anything." He smelled of sleep and morning sex and a hell of a lot of temptation. He wrapped his arms around her and pulled her into his warmth. "I love you."

"I love you too."

After a quick kiss, she stepped back, trying to leave his embrace, but he held on tight. "I have to go. If I'm late picking up Aya, she'll kill me."

"Move in with me. Please." He grinned and kissed her neck. "I'll wake you up every morning like I did today."

Her body trembled as she remembered the love they'd made less than an hour ago. "I just want to do things right this time, Aiden."

"This is right. You being here, in this house with me, is right."

"All right. I'll think about it." She laughed when he lifted her off her feet and spun her until he could lay her on the bed. "I have to go," she said when he started nipping at her neck.

He planted a kiss on her lips and then jumped up and trotted out of the room. "I'll call Phil. We'll take care of everything."

"Hey, I said I'd *think* about it," she called after him. She laughed lightly. She could try to deny it, but he was right. She'd always known that someday this would be her home. However, she wasn't expecting it to be quite this soon. Standing up, she fastened her pants and called to Aiden. "I'm leaving. Do *not* talk to Phil about this until we have a chance to discuss it further."

"Okay," he said above the noise of the shower.

Despite his words, she suspected he wasn't going to listen. She loved that man to the moon and back, but once he got something in his head, he didn't seem to want to hear anything else. She'd have to deal with his hardheadedness later though. She grabbed her bag and darted to her car. She had ten minutes to get to Aya's or they were going to be late.

She made it to Aya's in eight minutes. Two to spare. She didn't even have to get out of the car, Aya dashed out the front door of her condo and walked with quick, long strides to get into Meg's car.

"I was about to call you," Aya said. She settled in and let out an anxiety-laden sigh as she struggled with her seat belt. "I didn't bring any brushes. Was I supposed to bring brushes?"

"Nope. Kara has everything in her class." She backed out and glanced at her sister, who was clasping her hands together and fidgeting. "It's just a painting class, Aya. Don't look so scared."

Aya glanced at her and exhaled a heavy breath, but she only appeared more terrified. Meg didn't know if Aya had kept up with her painting, but she guessed that she hadn't. Art used to be so important to her. If she was nervous, that was okay. This was something she had always wanted to do. Meg was just happy she could be there with her as she took what Meg assumed was her first official art lesson.

"Aiden wants me to move in with him," Meg offered as a way of distraction.

Aya jerked her face to her sister. "That's a big step."

"I know. But it's also inevitable. I practically live there already. I go home every few days to trade out clothes and water my plants—which aren't surviving this transition very well at all." She smiled as she thought of the wilting snake plants she'd been neglecting. Even if she didn't move into Aiden's house right now, she needed to move her plants so they could get better care. "I'm scared, obviously. The last time didn't go so great. I'm not sure I should do it."

"Of course you should," Aya said.

Meg was surprised. She didn't think her sister would be so supportive. Aya had been easier to talk to lately and had been much more understanding of Meg's relationship, but she still hadn't expected her sister to encourage her to take such a big step with Aiden. "Yeah. I guess."

"You love him, right?"

"I do."

"I've seen how he looks at you. He loves you too. So…do it. Move in and give it a shot. If it doesn't work out, at least you tried. You have to try, Meg."

Meg's mind eased. She hadn't even considered that she'd need someone, especially Aya, to support her in making the decision. Now that she had that support, moving in with Aiden felt right. Just like he'd told her. It *was* right.

Meg parked on the street outside of Kara and Harry's house and led Aya to the little art studio that had been built in their backyard. That's where Kara held her lessons. Meg didn't really know where she found the time between Mira and being a midwife, but just like everything else, Kara always seemed to find a way.

"Hey, ladies," Meg called, and the group turned to face her. Most of them were her friends from work and knew Aya, which Meg was thankful for. Her sister struggled being around strangers sometimes, and she wanted this class to be as comfortable for Aya as possible.

The group of women all smiled and welcomed the new addition.

Meg and Aya sat side by side in front of blank canvases and a cup of brushes they would share.

"No laughing," Meg warned her. "I'm terrible at this."

Aya stopped taking in the scene to look at her. "Then why do you do it?"

"Because it's fun." Meg nudged her. "Don't you do anything just because it's fun?"

"No."

They laughed, but Meg knew she meant it. That was going to change. Meg would see to it. She had hoped that Aya's stiff posture and stressed expression would ease as they got into the class. Kara was the most laid-back teacher Meg had ever worked with. She had that whole Bob Ross "happy accidents" approach to art. Even if someone messed up in their eyes, she could help them get back on track with just a few pointers. However, as they continued painting, Aya's stress seemed to grow.

Meg looked at her sister's painting and exaggerated her approval. "Aya! That's amazing. How did you do that?"

Aya grinned, but the haunted look in her eyes remained. "I have a lot more practice than you. Remember? It's been a while, but it's coming back." She intently stared at Kara's brush as she instructed the little gathering on how to swish their brushes to make pine trees. As soon as Aya put the tip of her brush on the canvas, she stroked back and forth and perfectly imitated what Kara had done.

Meg tried, but her strokes were too thick and lopsided. "Always have to outshine me, don't you?" she teased.

Aya sat back and looked at Meg's painting, but her eyes glazed a bit and it was obvious she wasn't seeing the mess Meg had made. "So things with Aiden are going really well, then?"

The smile that spread on Meg's face practically hurt her cheeks.

"They're going great. Really, really great. We've both changed so much, but the base of our connection is still there. Does that make sense?"

"Yeah, it does. And his parents?"

Meg shrugged, guessing there'd always be a little bit of a cloud where his father was concerned. "His mother apologized, and I think she's really trying to show us that she accepts me. Maybe a little too much. She wants to take me shopping this week. That will be awkward since it will be the first time we've been together without Aiden there as a buffer, but I'm determined to make it work."

"And our parents?"

Something in Aya's voice piqued Meg's concern. "Better. I don't know that they will ever fully accept Aiden, but they were nice at dinner. Mom even asked how he was doing when she called the other day. Why?"

Aya looked to their instructor again and then easily, almost too naturally, created the tree trunk. She put her brush down and faced her sister, and something akin to fear filled her eyes.

Meg put her brush down too, but she grasped Aya's hand. "What? Did they say something to you?"

Aya shook her head. "No, but I... Meg, I..."

"What?"

"I need your help because I want to introduce someone to Mom and Dad too."

Meg sat a bit taller. "I didn't know you were dating." She laughed slightly. "Of course, Aya. You helped me so much. Of course I'll be there for you."

Aya stared at her. "You remember Tracy, don't you?"

Meg nodded. Aya's roommate was so sweet and bubbly. She seemed like the perfect person for Aya to be living with, even though they were opposites in many ways. Tracy cooked and cleaned up without saying too much about Aya's long work schedule. Aya had even said that Tracy had gone with her to look at a few houses. Meg wasn't sure but suspected once Aya bought a house, Tracy would move in with her and continue to be her roommate.

"Oh," Meg said with sudden realization. "*Tracy*. You and Tracy."

Aya nodded, her eyes wide and cheeks paled a shade or two, as if expecting her sister to freak out.

Instead, Meg offered her a great big reassuring smile. She didn't want her sister to fear, even for a moment, that she was judging or disapproving. It was Aya's choice to be with Tracy just like it was Meg's choice to be with Aiden. She'd never be anything less than supportive.

Squeezing her sister's hand, Meg said, "I love her, Aya. She's so nice, and she takes really great care of you."

A loud exhale rushed from Aya. "Mom and Dad aren't going to be so accepting."

Meg couldn't deny that. Her dad had proven that he wasn't so great at accepting his daughters choosing their own way, but if Meg had learned anything, it was that he had no control over what they chose. He only had control over how he dealt with their decisions.

"I think we can help them come around," Meg said. "I'll help you. Just like you helped me. I promise."

Aya blinked a few times and gave Meg what looked like the first real smile of the morning. Finally she relaxed, and Meg understood her tension hadn't been about the art class at all. She'd known going into the day that she was going to share her secret with Meg. She'd been scared. Meg hated that for her. She shouldn't have to worry about what people would think, but the reality was Aya would always face people who discriminated against her. Whether it was because of her race or her sexuality. Her heart hurt for her sister, and for herself, for the way some people chose to treat them.

"Will you and Tracy come to dinner soon? I'd like to get to know her better."

Aya seemed surprised, but she smiled. "I'd like that." Picking up her brush again, she caught up to where Kara was in her instructions without seeming to have to think about it. "How did you break through to Dad?" she asked after a few minutes.

Meg frowned at her failed attempt to make a bird. "Well, I told him that I'm happy with my choices and that if he couldn't accept Aiden, he couldn't accept me. And if I was forced to make a choice between him and Aiden, I'd choose Aiden. If Dad can't accept that you want to be with Tracy, then he can't accept you. It might take him some time, Aya, but I think he will. If he doesn't, that's his loss. You'll always have me."

Aya looked at the front of the little classroom, but she didn't seem to be listening to Kara explaining how to blend whites and grays to make clouds. "It's going to break his heart to find out I'm gay."

"It broke his heart when I dropped out of medical school. He'll get over it."

"He was angry for years, Meg."

"But he finally accepted it. And he'll accept you."

Aya sagged in her chair a little. "I hope so. We started talking about getting married. Not now," she added quickly when Meg gasped. "I mean, we're just talking about it."

Meg bit her lip but then confessed, "We've been talking about it too. Someday. We're not ready yet, but we will be. Oh my gosh. We have to coordinate so we don't have competing weddings. That would be awful."

Resting her hand on Meg's arm, Aya smiled. "Thank you. I was so worried to tell anyone."

Meg looked at her canvas. "What you should really be worried about is my painting skills. Look at this."

Giggling, Aya reached over with her brush. Somehow, having her clean up the mess Meg had made felt like balance had been restored between the sisters.

sh

"Take it easy on the stairs," Aiden warned when his brother stretched his legs, taking three steps in one despite the boxes in his arms.

"I got it," he said, dismissing his brother's warning.

Aiden had bribed him with pizza and cash to get him to help move Meg's stuff from her apartment to their house the following weekend. It was important to him that he and Stevie spend some time together, even if it was moving boxes. Aiden didn't think his dad would sink so low as to try to turn the brothers against each other, but Stevie had another year and a half before college, and Aiden didn't want the issues between him and his father to drift between him and his brother.

Aiden had no doubt Stevie was well aware of what was going on, but he acted oblivious. And he treated Meg with the same respect he'd treat anyone else, which made Aiden incredibly happy.

"How much more?" Aiden asked when Phil followed behind with two more boxes.

"Almost there."

Aiden chuckled. "How did she fit all this in that apartment?"

"Don't ask me," Phil said. "Women have magical powers for hoarding that I can't even begin to understand."

He went to the truck Phil had borrowed from Marcus and grabbed a few plastic containers that contained who knew what that were marked *closet* and headed upstairs. Mallory and Meg were putting the full drawers back into the chest of drawers that had come from Meg's apartment, confirming that all the boxes that were being carried in had come from her closet, kitchen, bathroom, and other areas. He again wondered where she'd kept all this stuff but decided not to ask.

"Here's more," he said to the two women in the walk-in closet.

"Are you kidding?" Aya muttered. She turned to her girlfriend. "We are not moving this much stuff."

"You say that now," Tracy countered. "But have you looked in your closet lately?"

Aya made a face as she finished hanging up the bundle of blouses in her arms.

Meg flashed Aiden a bright smile as he set the containers next to the closet. With all the helpers on hand, it wasn't long before the truck was empty. Aiden took charge of picking up lunch while Mallory and Meg continued settling her in. By the time Aiden returned, they were all ready to eat. For the first time since moving into the new house, Aiden saw a flaw in his plan.

He needed a bigger dining room table. There wasn't enough room for everyone to sit around it. That was something he and Meg would have to work on later. For now, he was happy to stand next to her at the kitchen counter while they listened to Phil and Stevie talk about a video game between bites of pizza. Mallory ate and simultaneously bounced the baby attached to her chest as she talked to Aya and Tracy. She'd become a master at multitasking, but Aiden worried she was setting herself up for the same kind of attachment issues Kara and Harry were just starting to break with Mira.

He wouldn't voice his concerns though. He'd learned that there were a lot worse things for a kid to have to get over than being loved too much. Wrapping his arm around Meg's shoulders, he tugged her close and kissed her head.

"You okay?" she asked.

"I'm perfect. You?"

"Absolutely perfect." Or at least he was until Meg stiffened and her eyes widened just a bit. He turned and froze as well.

His mother was standing in front of his father, looking scared and hopeful all at once. She held out what had become her signature peace offering of donuts.

"Hey," Aiden managed to say.

"You said you wanted a grill for the backyard," Becca offered. "Your father and I wanted to get a housewarming gift for you and Meg. I hope you don't mind, but we went and picked one out this morning."

His dad barely looked at Meg but did nod toward Aiden. "Where do you want it?"

"On the patio out back."

The man turned and disappeared, and Aiden thought everyone in the room let out a collective sigh of relief to see him go. Until Jim Howard disappeared, there seemed to have been no oxygen left in the room.

"He could probably use some help," Becca said pointedly to Aiden.

Meg looked up at him. "Go."

"Mom, if he starts anything..." he warned.

"Baby steps, Aiden. Okay? Let him take baby steps."

Aiden looked at the woman beside him. Meg nodded, and though he was hesitant, he left to go help his dad move a damn grill.

There was palpable tension between them as they lifted the box from the bed of his dad's truck and set it on a dolly. Aiden guided him as his dad steered the dolly through the garage and out to the backyard.

"Looks like a nice house," his dad offered as he used his pocket knife to cut open the box.

"It's nice. Not bad for a starter."

His dad pulled the box apart, and they worked on getting the grill set up, muttering about screws and screwdrivers and whether the handle went this way or that. They'd nearly completed the assembly when his dad said, "I was raised different is all. We didn't date people of different races."

"Stonehill didn't used to have people of different races, Dad. There wasn't anybody else *to* marry."

"Times are different," he said. "I know that. Your mom sure as hell has been beating me over the head with that lecture." He stood up. "Mom says you're going to marry her, maybe have some kids."

"That's my plan."

His dad nodded but didn't say anything else about it. Aiden guessed the man needed a bit more time to process that news. He didn't seem angry or upset; he just seemed to be letting the words sink in. When the grill was assembled, Jim folded up the box and stuffed it into the overflowing recycling bin. "That should do it." He stuck his head in the house. "All done, Bec. Let's go."

Aiden smiled at his mother as she rushed out. She paused long enough to cast him a worried glance. "It's fine, Mom," he assured her. "We're fine."

She made a point to call back into the house and tell Meg she'd see her soon before hugging Aiden. "Thank you."

"*Thank you.* I'm sure you had to twist his arm quite a few times to get that out of him."

"And withhold his dinner a few nights." She smiled and put her hand to his cheek. "He'll come around. It's just going to take some time."

"I know." He watched her hop into his dad's truck and waved as they backed out of the driveway. Inside, he went back to Meg and his now-cold pizza. "That was different."

"You okay?" she asked him.

"Yeah. Man, I'm starting to think this house is the *Twilight Zone*. Look at all the crazy things that happen here."

Meg laughed. "If your mom doesn't stop bringing donuts, though, we might have to kick her out again."

"So," Aya said, approaching the counter with two empty plates. "Think our parents will come around that fast?"

"I wouldn't exactly say that he's come around," Aiden said. "But he did keep his mouth shut, which is a big accomplishment."

"We'll take it," Meg said, clearly trying to boost Aiden's hopes that maybe someday soon, they could be a whole family with all the parts included.

Until then, as he looked around the room, he was amazed at how far his family had come and couldn't help but smile thinking of the little box he'd tucked into the back of his sock drawer. Inside the white box with the little red ribbon sat the most perfect diamond ring, just waiting for the right moment to come.

Soon, Aiden reminded himself. He looked out at the grill and thought how the weather was turning and before long they'd have a backyard filled with friends and family as he cooked burgers and hot dogs. Yeah. Soon. The perfect moment would come soon.

EPILOGUE

*M*usic and laugher filled the Stonehill Community Center as Aiden took Meg's hand, preparing to share their first dance as husband and wife. There were still strains, but Aiden supposed that was the price of having a close family. One that he would gladly pay. Their parents, Jim Howard included, were all there. Together.

Meg's parents were slowly coming around to Aya and Tracy's relationship. Very slowly. But they all had accepted that slow progress was still progress.

Pulling Meg against him, Aiden kissed her lightly. "I need to say something I've been thinking about all day."

"What?"

They swayed slowly to the same song they'd danced to years and years ago. "We're going to have ups and downs, but I promise to never let those downs get so low that either of us wants to leave. I'm going to make this work, no matter how hard it gets sometimes."

She smiled. "*We* will. This is a team effort."

"And we make a hell of a team."

"Yes, we do."

As they slowly spun, Aiden hugged her close and took in the room filled with the people they loved.

Kara and Harry laughed as Mira and Jessica danced in front of them. Mira was getting a bit more comfortable putting some distance between her and her parents, but Aiden saw how she continually looked at them, making sure they were close and watching. Kara put her arm around Harry's shoulder, and he looked at her with so much love it made Aiden smile. They shared a kiss but only had a moment before Mira demanded they return her attention to her.

Dianna and Paul O'Connell shared a dance of their own, lost in each other as they tended to be.

Jessica laughed as Phil took her hand and spun her. Mallory smiled as she looked on, surprisingly without baby Harris attached to her. Annie held her grandson as Marcus sat close, admiring his family. That included Jenna and Daniel, who hadn't earned a single tense look from Marcus all day. Of course, how could Marcus glare at him when Daniel was clearly so enamored with Jenna and their daughter? Little Lily was bundled in pink and sound asleep in her mama's arms.

His mother and father sat at the next table. They weren't talking, but they were there. His mother had helped plan the wedding, which Aiden and Meg had appreciated. His father dropped by occasionally, usually to fix something without saying much, and then he'd leave. But it was something, and Aiden would take it. Stevie had his nose is his phone, but he was present for his brother's wedding and that was all he and Meg expected.

As they turned, Aiden whispered for Meg to look at the table where her parents, sister, and Tracy were sitting. Eiji Tanaka held his usual stiff posture, but he was talking to Aya and Tracy, which was not something he had appeared interested in doing previously. Meg looked up at Aiden and grinned.

"Baby steps," he said, reminding her of his mother's suggestion where his father was concerned.

Meg laughed lightly and dragged her finger down his cheek. "Speaking of baby steps..."

His heart dropped to this stomach as she let the implication linger between them. "Wait. Are you?"

"We're having a baby."

He stared at her as he realized this was everything he had been working for. This moment, this little blip in time was everything. He had Meg. He had his family. And they were having a baby. Aiden let out a whoop as he scooped her up against him.

"We're having a baby," he yelled, setting off a chorus of cheers.

ALSO BY MARCI BOLDEN

STONEHILL SERIES:

The Road Leads Back

Friends Without Benefits

The Forgotten Path

Jessica's Wish

This Old Café

Forever Yours

OTHER TITLES:

Unforgettable You (coming soon)

A Life Without Water (coming soon)

ABOUT THE AUTHOR

As a teen, Marci Bolden skipped over young adult books and jumped right into reading romance novels. She never left.

Marci lives in the Midwest with her husband, kiddos, and numerous rescue pets. If she had an ounce of willpower, Marci would embrace healthy living, but until cupcakes and wine are no longer available at the local market, she will appease her guilt by reading self-help books and promising to join a gym "soon."

Visit her here:
www.marcibolden.com

 facebook.com/MarciBoldenAuthor

twitter.com/BoldenMarci

instagram.com/marciboldenauthor

CPSIA information can be obtained
at www.ICGtesting.com
Printed in the USA
FSHW010155071120
75621FS